V.C. ANDREWS®

Cinnamon

G.K. Hall & Co. • Waterville, Maine

Published in 2002 by arrangement with Pocket Books, a division of Simon & Schuster.

G.K. Hall Large Print Core Series.

The text of this Large Print edition is unabridged.
Other aspects of the book may vary from the original edition.

Set in 16 pt. Plantin by Myrna S. Raven.

Printed in the United States on permanent paper.

Library of Congress Cataloging-in-Publication Data

Andrews, V. C. (Virginia C.)
    Cinnamon / V.C. Andrews
        p. cm.
    ISBN 0-7838-9750-2 (lg. print : hc : alk. paper)
    1. Mothers and daughters — Fiction.   2. Young women — Fiction.   3. Actresses — Fiction.   4. Large type books.   I. Title.
PS3551.N454 C56 2002
    813'.54—dc21   2001051696

Cinnamon

Prologue

"Cinnamon Carlson."

I was just as surprised as everyone else to hear Miss Hamilton call out my name. Edith Booth, the student hall monitor and everyone's candidate for this year's Miss Goody Two-shoes, had just interrupted our English literature class. She had opened the door and tapped her perfect little steps across the hardwood floor while walking with flawless posture. Her shoulders were pulled back firmly, and an invisible book was on top of her clump of dull brown hair, hair that everyone knew her mother trimmed unevenly at the base of her neck and around her ears.

She had looked in my direction as soon as she had entered the classroom and then handed Miss Hamilton the note from the principal's office as if it were a speeding ticket or an eviction notice. I wanted to crack an egg over that smug, arrogant little smile she had pasted on her face.

Miss Hamilton's face was already flushed with crimson frustration at the interruption. She had just gotten into the flow of Desdemona's pathetic defense right before Othello was about to smother her to death with a pillow. Even some of the zombies in class, as

7

Clarence Baron and I liked to refer to them, were glued to her performance. What could you expect? It was practically the only live theater some of them had ever experienced.

After having once made a futile effort to become an actress, Miss Hamilton had fallen back into a teaching career like someone who had tried to ski professionally and quickly found herself on her rear end gliding down into mediocrity. She spent the rest of her young adult life gazing wistfully at the skiers who went gracefully beyond her. Now, in the role of the school's drama coach, she dreams of being the inspiration, the greatest influence on the next Meryl Streep or Jodie Foster. Lately, she's been eyeing me, urging me to try out for the school play, which was something Mommy thought I should do as well because of the role-playing she and I often perform in the attic of our house.

"You're so good at it, Cinnamon," she would tell me. "Someday, you'll be a wonderful actress."

You have to be a wonderful actress or actor to survive in this world, I thought. Controlling your face, your voice, your posture and most of all being able to invent reasons and excuses to answer questions are the real skills of self-defense. To me, especially lately, going out in the world with honesty on your lips was the same as going out naked.

I looked up when I heard the door open and

Miss Hamilton pause. While she had been reciting her Desdemona, I had kept my eyes glued to the top of my desk. Her over-the-top histrionics was embarrassing to watch, and I really liked *Othello*. Listening to Miss Hamilton read it was similar to being forced to observe someone ruin a good recipe for crème brûlée. Everyone who hadn't eaten the dessert before would think this was it, this terrible tasting stuff was it? They would never ask for it again.

I knew instinctively that Desdemona at this point in the play should still not believe it was possible Othello would kill her. Her voice should ring with disbelief, innocence, love and faith. Why didn't Miss Hamilton know that, or if she did, why couldn't she express it?

How many times had Shakespeare spun in his grave?

I liked Miss Hamilton, probably more than any of my other teachers, but I was never good at overlooking faults. I always flip over the brightest coin and look at the tarnish.

"Your grandmother is waiting for you at Mr. Kaplan's office," Miss Hamilton said.

I looked back at Clarence Baron who was practically the only one my age with whom I communicated these days. I hesitated to call him my boyfriend. We hadn't crossed that line yet and I was still not sure at the time if we ever would. That wasn't because I thought he was unattractive. Quite the contrary. He had an interesting face with dark, lonely eyes that revealed not only his sensitivity but also his intelligence. He kept his chocolate brown hair long and unruly, full of wild curls. I knew he thought it made him resemble Ludwig van Beethoven, not that Clarence had any interest in composing music. He just enjoyed classical music and knew more about it than anyone else I knew.

He was slim, almost too thin for his six feet one inch height, but I liked his angular jaw and nearly perfect nose over a strong full mouth. I've overheard girls often commenting about him, always saying things like "Too bad he's so weird. He's sexy."

I knew why they thought he was weird. He admitted that he couldn't help doing what he called his rituals. For example, Clarence was in the last seat in the first row. It was a very important thing for him to take the same seat in all of his classes, if he could. I suppose it was really compulsion. Another ritual was never leaving a building on an odd step. He counted his steps toward the exit and always made sure he walked out on an even number. I've often seen him stop and go back just to be sure. He also eats everything on his dinner plate from left to right, no matter what it is, and he's right-handed! He even manages to do it with pasta. I don't ask him why he does these strange things anymore. If I did, he would just say, "It feels right," or he would shrug and say, "I don't know why, Cinnamon. I just do it."

Clarence raised his heavy, dark brown eyebrows into question marks and I sucked in my breath and shook my head.

I had no idea why my grandmother was coming to take me out of school, but I did have fears boiling under the surface of my confusion.

Two days ago, Mommy had suffered her second miscarriage. After the first miscarriage eight years ago, she and Daddy seemed to have given up on having another child. I even harbored the belief that they had stopped having sex. Rarely did I see them express any passion toward each other, especially after Grandmother Beverly had moved in with us. A peck on the cheek, a quick embrace or a brush of hands was generally all I witnessed, not that I spied on my parents or anything. It was just an observation of something that had settled into their lives and mine, seeping through our days like a cold, steady rain.

So I was just as surprised as my grandmother when one day a little more than six months ago, Mommy made the announcement at dinner.

After swallowing a piece of bread, she released a deep sigh and said, "Well, I'm pregnant again."

Grandmother Beverly, who had moved in with us shortly after Grandfather Carlson had died, dropped her fork on the plate, nearly breaking the dish. She turned and looked at my father as if he had betrayed some trust, some agreement in blood they had signed.

"At her age?" she asked him. "She's going to have another child now?" She turned to my mother, who had always had the ability to ignore Grandmother Beverly, to seem not to hear her or see her whenever she wanted, even if she was sitting or standing right in front of her. She could go as deaf and as stony as a marble statue. Of course, that made Grandmother Beverly even angrier.

"You're forty-two years old, Amber. What are you thinking?" she snapped with her same old authority.

Grandmother Beverly has never hesitated to express her opinions or make her demands. My grandfather had been a meek, gentle man whose strongest criticism or chastisement of her was a shaking of his head and only twice at that. He went left to right, left to right and stopped with a shrug and that was always the extent of his resistance. No arguments, no pouts, no rants or raves or anything added. Once, when I tried to describe him to Clarence, I dryly said, "Think of him as Poland after Hitler's invasion."

It was not difficult for me to think of Grandmother Beverly as a ruthless dictator.

"What I'm thinking," Mommy replied slowly to Grandmother Beverly's question, "is that I'll give birth to a healthy child. Besides, it's not so uncommon these days for a woman my age to give birth. I recently read where a woman in her fifties got pregnant. And not as a surrogate mother either," she quickly added.

Grandmother Beverly's eyes darkened and narrowed with disapproval. She picked up her fork and returned to her methodical eating, gazing furiously at my father who busied himself with cutting his steak. After that, silence boomed in our ears as loudly as Beethoven's Fifth Symphony.

However, silence was no sign of surrender when it came to my grandmother. She never missed an opportunity to express her disapproval. All through Mommy's months of pregnancy, Grandmother Beverly nagged and nipped at her like a yapping poodle. As soon as Mommy started to show, Grandmother's complaints intensified.

"A woman your age walking around in maternity clothes," she barked. "What a sight you must make. You even have some strands of gray in your hair, and now you have to watch what you eat more than ever. Women at your age gain weight more easily. You'll end up looking like my sister Lucille who popped children out like a rabbit and ended up resembling a baby elephant. Her hips grew so big, she once got stuck in a chair," Grandmother emphasized, looking at me and nodding.

Whenever she couldn't get a reaction from Mommy, she would try directing herself at me as if I were a translator who would explain what she had said.

"Aunt Lucille has only three children, doesn't she?" I asked.

"That's too many," Grandmother Beverly replied so quickly anyone would have thought she and I had rehearsed the dialogue. "Children are expensive and difficult nowadays. They make you years older than you are in short order. They need, need, need. When I was a child, the word *want* did not exist. My mouth was stuffed with 'please' and 'thank you' and 'no sir' and 'yes ma'am' and that was that. I can't even imagine my father's reaction to my asking him for a new dress or a car or money to waste on silly jewelry. Why if he was alive today and saw some of those . . . I don't know what you call them . . . walking around with rings in their noses and in their belly buttons, he'd think the world had come to an end and rightly so."

"Well, they'll be only two children in this house," I said and looked at Mommy. She was trying hard not to pay attention, but Grandmother Beverly was wearing her down, her snipping words coming at her from every direction like a pack of hyenas. By now Mommy was full of aches and pains and too pale, I thought.

And then she suffered the miscarriage. She started to hemorrhage one night and had to be rushed to the hospital. I woke to the sounds of her screams and panic. Daddy wouldn't let me

14

go along. He came home alone hours and hours later and announced she had lost the baby.

Grandmother Beverly felt no guilt or sorrow. Her reaction was to claim it was Nature's way of saying no to something that shouldn't have been begun in the first place. When they brought Mommy home the day after, Mommy couldn't bear to look at her. She didn't look at anyone very much for that matter, not even me. Her eyes were distant, her sorrow shutting her up tightly, a prisoner in her own body.

Now I trembled inside imagining the possible reasons for my grandmother's very unexpected arrival at school.

Quickly closing my copy of *Othello* and my notebook, I gathered all of my things and rose. I knew everyone in the class was watching me, their eyes loyally following my every gesture, but most of my life I've felt people's eyes on me. It doesn't bother me anymore. In fact, it probably never did or at least never as much as it should. That indifference, or that dramatic *fourth wall,* as Miss Hamilton likes to call it, was always up, always between me and the rest of the world whenever I wanted it to be. In that sense I'm really like Mommy, although I must say, Daddy can be deaf and dumb at the drop of a nasty word, too. He certainly was that way more often around Grandmother Beverly these days.

I know that people, including some of my

teachers and especially my grandmother, would say I deliberately attract attention because of the way I dress and behave. My auburn hair is thick and long, down to my shoulder blades. I won't cut it any shorter than that and barely trim my bangs. Sometimes, strands fall over my eyes or over one eye and I leave them there, looking out at the world, my teachers, other students, everything and everyone through a sheer, rust-tinted curtain. I know it unnerves some people and especially drives Grand-mother Beverly to the point where her pallid face takes on crimson blotches at the crests of her bony cheeks.

"Cut your hair or at least have the decency to brush it back neatly. I can't tell if you're looking at me or what when I speak to you," she often carped. One criticism led to another. She was a spider weaving its web. "And don't you have anything cheerful to wear to school?"

Like Mommy, I favor dark colors. I'm always dressed in black or dark blue, often dark gray, and I put on a translucent white lipstick and black nail polish. I darken my eyebrows and wear too much eyeshadow, and I keep out of the sun, not only because I know it damages your skin, but I like having a light complexion. My skin is so transparent, I can see tiny blue veins in my temples, and I think about my blood moving through these tiny wires to my heart and my brain.

At the moment, my heart felt as though it

had been put on pause.

Edith Booth waited for me at the classroom door. She was performing her role as hall monitor, which meant she would escort me out and to the principal's office like some military parade guard. She pressed her thin, crooked lips together and pulled her head up, tightening her neck and her chin. She held the door open, but as I walked through it, I reached back, seized the knob and pulled it hard out of her hands, slamming it behind me.

I could hear the class roar at the sight of her staring into the shut door, her jaw probably dropped, her perfect posture definitely ruined. I heard her fumbling with the knob and then come charging out, flustered, rushing to catch up with me, her heels clicking like an explosion of small firecrackers on the tile corridor floor.

"That wasn't very nice," she said.

I turned and glared at her.

Everyone who knows us and who has seen our house thinks the spirits inside the house will eventually drive us all mad. They think it's haunted. They call it "The Addams Family House." The outside is so dark and it does have this foreboding presence. I actually believe Daddy is ashamed of his house. Grandmother Beverly certainly didn't want him to buy it, but that was one time Mommy won out over her when it came to having Daddy decide something. Mommy was determined.

It's a grand Second Empire Victorian house

about ten miles northwest of Tarrytown, New York. The original owner was a former Civil War officer who had served under General Grant. His name was Jonathan Demerest and he had five children, two boys and three girls. Both his wife Carolyne and his youngest son Abraham died of smallpox less than a year apart. Their graves, as well as Jonathan's, are on our property, up on a knoll from where you could once see miles and miles in any direction. At least that's what Mommy claimed. She said when they first moved into the house, the forest wasn't anywhere as grown as it is today; of course, there weren't all those houses in one development after another peppering the face of the landscape like pimples.

"It was a peaceful place, a wonderful place to be buried," she told me. "It still is, actually. Maybe I should be buried here, too," she added and I cried because I was only nine at the time and I didn't want to hear about such a thing as my own mother's death.

"We all die, Cinnamon," she said with that soft, loving smile that could always bring my marching heart back to a slow walk. She would touch my cheek so gently, her fingers feeling like a warm caressing breeze, and she would smile a smile full of candlelight, warm, mesmerizing. "It's not that bad when our time comes. We just move on," she said looking out at the world below us as if she already had one foot in the grave. "We just move on to somewhere quieter. That's all."

"Quieter? How could it be any quieter than this?" I wondered aloud.

"It's quieter inside you," she replied. I didn't understand what that meant for years, but now I do.

I really do.

Anyway, Mommy told me she had fallen in love with our house before she had fallen in love with Daddy, and she got him to buy it after only a year of marriage.

The house appears larger than it really is because it was built on a hill and looms over the roads and homes below us. It has three stories with a cupola that looks like a great hiding place for a monster or a ghost. Some of the kids think I crawl up into it every night and send spells and curses down on unwary travelers below. Whenever I hear these kinds of things about myself, I laugh, toss back my hair and say what Mommy told me Katharine Hepburn once said about publicity: "I don't care what they say about me, as long as it isn't true."

Very few people understand what that means. They think it's just more proof of my weirdness. They don't understand that when people invade your life and uncover the truth about you, they expose things you want to keep private, keep personal so you can keep your self-respect. It's why we lock our doors and close our windows and pull down our shades, especially in my house.

19

I don't care what impression my house makes on people. I love it as much as Mommy does. Second Empire houses have what are known as mansard roofs, which are roofs having two slopes on all sides with the lower slope steeper than the upper one. The house itself is square, and it has elaborate decorative iron cresting above the upper cornice. The front of the house has paired entry doors with glass in the top half and a half-dozen steps leading up and under the one-story porch. All of the windows are paired. The downstairs ones are all hooded. Mommy loves talking about it, lecturing about the architecture to anyone who will listen.

Grandmother Beverly thought it was a dreadful place to live, even though she readily moved in with us. Mommy said it was Grand-mother Beverly's sole idea to move in, despite Daddy's telling me and everyone else that he asked her to move in with us since we had so much room and there was no reason for a woman of her age to have to live alone.

"No reason," Mommy told me, "except to give us peace of mind."

Anyway people often look at me as if they expect that any day now — because we live in the eerie looking, supposedly haunted house — I'll become a raving lunatic and maybe even try to hurt myself. Even when some of my teachers talk to me, I notice they stand a foot or so farther away from me than they stand away from their other students. All I have to do sometimes is stare at someone the way I was staring at Edith Booth and I can see him or her suddenly become overwhelmed with small terrors. The truth is, I've begun to enjoy it. It gives me a sense of power.

"What?" I snapped at her.

She stepped back.

"Mr. Kaplan . . . wants you . . . right away," she stuttered.

"Then stop interrupting me," I ordered. I locked my eyes onto hers and the color fled her cheeks.

She remained a few feet behind me all the way to the principal's office where I found Grandmother Beverly sitting anxiously on the small, imitation leather settee. She was rubbing her fingers in her palm as if she were trying to sand down some imaginary calluses, something she often did when she was very nervous.

The moment I entered the outer office, she rose to her full five feet four inches of height. Grandfather Carlson had been six feet two inches tall, but he always looked diminished in her presence, and Daddy never seems his full six feet next to her either. Her shadow shrinks people.

"Stature comes from your demeanor, your self-confidence," Mommy once told me when we talked about Grandmother Beverly. "You've got to give the devil her due for that."

Mommy was practically the only person I knew who wasn't intimidated by her, but she

21

wasn't strong enough to do constant battle with her, not with what I've come to think of as the Trojan Horse in our home, my own father. He could be strong in so many ways, but when it came to facing down his own mother, he became a little boy again.

For instance, Grandmother Beverly was as critical of the inside of our house as she was of the outside. She hated Mommy's taste in decorations, furniture, curtains, flooring, even lighting and bathroom fixtures. From the moment she moved in, she seemed determined to slowly change it all. She would point out the smallest imperfection, a tiny stain in a chair, a tear in a rug, and advised Daddy to have it replaced. Once he agreed to that, she went forward to choose what the replacement would be, as if Mommy wasn't even there.

One day a chair would be supplanted or a rug, and when Mommy complained that what Grandmother Beverly had chosen didn't mesh with our decor, Daddy would plead and moan and promise that after this or that there would be no more changes. Of course, there always were.

It was easy to see why I compared Grandmother's march through our house and lives to Hitler's march through Europe. Daddy was our own little Chamberlain promising "Peace for our time," if we just made one more compromise. Then we would be a happy little family again.

That's something we would never be again.

But I didn't know how definite that prophecy was until I went home from school with Grandmother Beverly.

1

Darkness Descends

"What's wrong? Why have you come for me?" I asked her.

Once I had arrived, she had simply started out of the principal's office and begun her stomp through the corridor to the exit for the parking lot. As usual she expected me to trail along like some obedient puppy.

She continued to walk, ignoring my questions. She always fixed herself on her purpose or destination as if she were a guided missile. Getting her to pause, turn or stop required the secret abort code only her own private demon knew and was reluctant to relinquish or reveal. You just had to wait her out, calm yourself down and be patient as difficult as that was. Grandmother Beverly could spread droplets of poison frustration on everyone around her like a lawn sprinkler.

But this was different. She had ripped me out of school and sent my head spinning. I would not be denied.

"Grandmother?"

"Just let's get out of here," she said sharply, not looking at me. She lowered her voice and added, "I don't want anyone hearing about this, if I can help it."

My heart was racing now, galloping alongside my unbridled imagination.

"Your foolish father," she muttered. "I warned him. No one can say I didn't warn him."

We passed through the doors and headed toward her vintage Mercedes sedan.

"Grandmother," I cried, planting my feet firmly in the parking lot. "I'm not taking another step until you tell me exactly what is going on."

She paused finally and turned to me, hoisting those small shoulders like a cobra preparing for a deadly strike.

"Your mother has gone mad and you're the only one who can talk to her. I certainly can't. Of course, I can't reach your father," she said, "and there's no time to wait for him anyway. I don't want to call an ambulance if I can help it."

"Ambulance?"

"You know how one thing leads to another and in this community there's enough gossip about this family as it is," she continued. "Maybe you can get her to stop."

"Stop what?"

"I can't even begin to describe it," she said, wagging her head as if her hair had been soaked. "Let's just get home," she insisted and hurried to get into the car. Now that she had sharpened my curiosity and raised the level of my anxiety like mercury in a thermometer, I rushed to get in as well.

Once I was seated, my head bowed with the panic I felt.

"I must tell you," she continued after starting the engine and pulling away from the school parking lot, "I have always felt your mother was unbalanced. She had tendencies I spotted from the first moment I set eyes on her. I warned Taylor about her minutes after he had brought her around for me and your grandfather to meet her.

"She was coming to see us for the first time, but she wore no makeup, draped herself in what looked to be little more than a black sheet, kept her hair miles too long like you do and had enough gloom in her eyes to please a dozen undertakers. She could have worked constantly as a professional mourner. I could count on my fingers how many times I've seen a smile on that face, and even if she did smile at me, it was the smile of a madwoman, her eyes glittering like little knives, her wry lips squirming back and into the corners of her cheeks like worms in pain. How many times have I asked myself what he could possibly have seen in such a woman?"

I had heard a similar lecture before.

"Maybe he was in love, Grandmother."

"Love," she spat as if the word put a bitter taste in her mouth. "How could he be in love with her?"

She glanced at me and then put her eyes back on the road. She was a good driver for someone in her early seventies, I thought, but then again, she was good at everything she did. Failure wasn't in her personal vocabulary.

"Your mother was certainly never what I would call beautiful. I'm not saying she doesn't have pleasing features, because she does, but she does nothing to enhance them. In fact, what she does is diminish them just like you do with that silly makeup you wear.

"Of course, it didn't help that she had the personality of a pallbearer. Believe me," she said, "that takes the light from your eyes, the glow from your smile. It's no wonder to me that she never made any friends. Who wants to listen to the music she likes or read those poems about loss and death and insanity? She has no social graces, doesn't care about nice clothes or jewelry. She was never interested in your father's work or helped him meet business associates."

"Then what do you think it was, Grand-mother," I asked dryly, "a magic spell?"

"You think you're being facetious, I know, but let me tell you that woman can cast spells of sorts. I'll tell you what it was," she said, after a short pause, never wanting to admit to not knowing something. "She was probably his first love affair. Men, foolish men, often mistake sexual pleasure for love. Sex is like good food. You can eat it with anyone, Cinnamon. Remember that," she ordered.

"Then what's love?" I asked her.

"Love is commitment, responsibility, dedication. It requires maturity."

"Sounds boring," I said. "If that's love, I'll take good food."

She opened her mouth wide and glared at me, shaking her head.

"You'd better be careful of your thoughts," she admonished. "Insanity can be inherited, you know. The genes from our side of the family just might not be enough."

I wanted to laugh at her, but I kept thinking about what awaited me and how it might make her right.

No one could tell anything about the inhabitants of our home by simply driving up, especially this time of the day. The front faced east so that all morning the windows were turned into glittering slabs, impenetrable crystals, twisting, turning and reflecting the sunlight. In fact, if it wasn't a day for the gardeners, and today wasn't, there was a look of abandonment about the place. Our cars were always left in the rear, out of sight. Two tall weeping willows on the northeast end painted long shadows over one side of the structure, adding to the sense of desertion.

There was a swing under a maple tree to the right on the west side. I noticed it was going back and forth, which made me smile. Anyone looking at it would be convinced there was a ghost sitting on it. I imagined one myself, one of the Demerest girls, smiling.

Fall had just lifted its head and begun to blow the cooler winds over the landscape, waving a magical hand to change the greens into yellows, browns and oranges. The grass, however, seemed happier, waking to heavier dews every morning. It was a deeper green. I loved the aroma of freshly cut lawns, the fresh-ness traveled into my brain and washed away the cobwebs and shadows from my darker thoughts.

As Grandmother Beverly turned up the drive, she finally revealed the situation in detail.

"I was in the living room, watching a good Cary Grant movie, when I heard her humming in the hallway. What is she doing downstairs? I wondered. The doctor had specifically told her that if she was going home, she was to remain in bed, resting, getting stronger. I offered to be her nurse, to march up and down those stairs as many times as need be, so she couldn't use that as any excuse.

"But your mother never listens to wiser voices. She hears only what she wants to hear. Secret voices out of the shadows," she mut-tered.

"Anyway, I went to the family room doorway. At first, I didn't see her. Then I heard her talking to her plants."

She paused, smirked and shook her head.

Mommy often spoke aloud to her plants as if they were her little children. She said when she was sad, which was far too often, the leaves were limp and dreary, but when she was happy, they were crisp and alive.

Anyway, I didn't think much of that.

"She's always talking to flowers, Grandmother. Many people do that."

"Naked?"

"What?"

"She was standing there in the hallway, watering those plants naked, and she was using a bed pan to water them," she said, her voice rising. "Who even knows if it was water?"

I felt the blood drain a bit from my face and looked at the house as we started around back.

"But that wasn't the horror of it, Cinnamon. 'What are you doing, Amber?' I asked, and she turned slowly toward me, a crazed smile on her face."

Grandmother stopped the car and turned to me before shutting off the engine.

"Over her stomach, with a stick of red lipstick, she had drawn the outline of a baby, a fetus!" she cried with a grimace. "I screamed, 'Oh, my God!' I nearly fainted at the sight, but she continued to smile at me and then went back to watering the plants, humming and watering.

"So, I got into the car and went for you."

I swallowed back the rock that had risen into my throat and got out of the car. All I could think of was Ophelia's mad scene in *Hamlet*. With my head down, my feet feeling like they had turned into marshmallows, I charged toward the rear entrance and quickly went inside, through the rear entryway and down the corridor to the stairway, gazing in each room to be sure Mommy wasn't downstairs.

Then I pounded up the stairs and paused when I reached the top. I could hear her humming and talking to herself. It was coming from the room that had been set up to be the nursery. Slowly, I approached it and looked in. It was just as Grandmother Beverly had described: Mommy was naked, the imaginary baby crudely drawn over her stomach in her apple red lipstick.

She was folding and unfolding the same little blanket at the side of the bassinet.

"Mommy," I said.

She stopped humming and looked at me.

"Cinnamon, you're home. Good. I was having labor pains this morning. It won't be long now," she said.

"Labor pains? But Mommy —"

"It's expected, I know, but it's still very difficult, Cinnamon. Most wonderful things are difficult," she muttered, "and worth the pain," she added with a new smile.

How could she have forgotten she had just had a miscarriage? It was so sad, so tragic, I thought, and then: Maybe that's why she's forgotten. She doesn't want to remember. She and

31

I have done so much pretending in this house. This comes easily to her.

"Mommy, you've got to return to bed."

"I will as soon as I do this. I want everything to be ready when we come home with little Sacha," she said, gazing around the nursery.

"Come back to bed, Mommy," I said, moving to her. I gently took her by the elbow. She smiled at me and put the blanket in the bassinet.

"My grown-up little lady, taking care of me. You're going to be such a big help with Sacha, I know. I'm as happy for you as I am for Daddy and me," she said. "Did you know I always wished I had a sister, especially a little sister who would look up to me for everything?

"Sacha's going to idolize you, Cinnamon. She'll want to do everything you do just the way you do it, I'm sure. You mustn't be short with her or impatient," she warned, her face full of concern. "Always remember she's just a little girl who doesn't understand. Explain things; make sure you and she always talk and never hide anything from each other. A sister can be your best friend in the whole world, even more than your mother. I'm sure mine would have been."

She started out with me, but she didn't stop talking.

"It's all right for her to be a better friend to you than I am. I'll never be jealous of the two of you, honey. I realize you will have more in common with her than you will with me. You don't ever have to worry about that."

"Please get into bed, Mommy," I said when we entered the master bedroom.

Mommy and Daddy had a king-size, oak four-post bed with an oversized headboard on which two roses with their stems crossed were embossed. Mommy loved roses. The comforter and the pillow cases had a pattern of red roses, which made the room cheerful. When they were younger and more affectionate toward each other, I used to think of their bed as a bed that promised its inhabitants magical love, a bed that filled their heads with wonderful dreams when they slept afterward, both of them, smiling, contented, warm and secure, those four posts like powerful arms protecting them against any of the evil spirits that sought to invade their contentment.

I pulled back the comforter and she got into the bed, slowly lowering her head to the pillow. She was still smiling.

"I want you to help take care of her right from the start, honey. You'll be her second mother, just as Agatha Demerest was a second mother to her younger brothers and sisters," she said. "Remember?"

Mommy was referring to a story she and I had actually created during one of our earliest visits to the attic.

When I was a little more than fourteen, she decided one day that we should explore the house. She had been up in the attic before, of course, and told me that shortly after she and Daddy had moved into the house, she had discovered an old hickory chest with hinges so rusted, they fell off when she lifted the lid. The chest was filled with things that went back to the 1800s. She had been especially intrigued by the Demerest family pictures. Most were faded so badly you could barely make out the faces, but some of them were still in quite good condition.

Daddy, who works on Wall Street and puts a monetary value on everything in sight, decided that much of the stuff could be sold. He took things like the Union army uniform, old newspapers, a pair of spurs and a pistol holster to New York to be valued and later placed in a consignment store, but Mommy wouldn't let him take the pictures.

"I told him family pictures don't belong in stores and certainly don't belong on the walls of strangers. These pictures should never leave this house and they never will," she vowed to me.

She and I would look at the women and the men and try to imagine what they must have been like, whether they were sad or happy people, whether they suffered or not. We did our role-playing and I would assume the persona of one of the women in a picture. Mommy would often be Jonathan Demerest, speaking in a deep voice. That was when we came up with the story of Agatha Demerest having to take on the role of mother when her mother died of smallpox.

But Mommy was talking about it now as if it were historical fact and we had no concrete information upon which to base our assumptions, except for the dates carved in a couple of tombstones.

"Okay, Mommy," I said. I was thinking about washing the lipstick drawing off her stomach, but I was afraid even to mention it.

I have to try to get in touch with Daddy, I thought.

"Oh," Mommy suddenly cried. "Oh, oh, oh, Cinnamon, it's happening again!" She clutched her stomach. "It's getting worse. I'm going into labor. You'd better call the doctor, call an ambulance, call your father," she cried.

She released a chilling scream that shook my very bones.

"Hurry!"

I didn't know what to do. I ran from the room. Grandmother Beverly was already at the top of the stairway.

"What is it?" she asked, her hand on her breast, her face whiter than ever.

"She thinks she's in labor. I think she really is in pain!"

"Oh dear, dear. We'll have to call the doctor. I was hoping you could calm her down, get her to sleep and be sane," she said. Another scream from Mommy spun her around and sent her fleeing down the stairway.

Mommy continued to moan.

I glanced at my watch. Daddy had to be at his desk. Why did Grandmother Beverly say before that she certainly couldn't reach him? He should be easy to reach.

I rushed to my room and tapped out the number for his office quickly. It rang and rang until his secretary finally picked up and announced his company.

"I need to speak to my father immediately," I practically screamed.

Mommy was crying out even louder now, her shouts of pain echoing down the hallway and through the house.

"He's not here at the moment," the secretary said.

"But he has to be. The market is still open."

"I'm sorry," she said.

"Where is he?"

"He didn't leave a number," she said.

"It's an emergency," I continued.

"Let me see if he answers his page," she relented. Why hadn't she said that first? I wondered. I held on, my heart pounding a drum in my ears.

"I'm sorry," she said. "He's not responding."

"Keep trying and if you get him, tell him my mother is being taken to the hospital."

"The hospital? Oh, dear. Oh," she said. "Yes, I'll keep trying."

I hung up just as Grandmother Beverly came

up the stairs, looking more her age.

"The doctor has called the ambulance," she said. She swallowed and continued. "It's no use. She has to return to the hospital. When I told him what she had done, he said he'd have her brought to the mental ward."

"Mental ward?"

"Of course. Look at her behavior. That's exactly where she belongs," she added with that damnable look of self-satisfaction I hated so much.

She put her hands over her ears, but Mommy's heart-wrenching scream drove Grandmother Beverly back down the stairs to wait.

I was hoping it would drive her out of our lives.

2

Escape to Dreams

Apparently, Daddy's secretary was unable to reach him before the ambulance arrived. I returned to Mommy's bedroom and held her hand while she went through her imaginary labor pains. I guess I shouldn't say imaginary. The doctor would emphasize later that she actually felt the pain.

"Psychosomatic pain is not contrived," he explained to Daddy when Daddy and I met with him in the corridor of the hospital. "The patient feels it; it's just caused by something psychological as compared to something physical." He looked at me and added, "We shouldn't get angry at her."

"I'm not angry at her," I snapped back at him. "I'm upset."

I almost added, I'm frightened, too, but he got me so angry I didn't want to confide in him.

Afterward, Daddy and I sat in the hospital cafeteria having a cup of coffee. Daddy said he hadn't had a chance to eat anything so he nibbled on a Danish pastry.

"When my secretary reached me, I was on

my way home," he told me. "I stopped at the train station and called and Grandmother answered and told me what was happening so I came back as quickly as I could and took a cab here. Lucky Grandmother was still in the house."

"It wasn't luck. Grandmother didn't want to come along. I drove myself and followed the ambulance. I'm sure she was afraid she might be seen by one of her society friends," I muttered.

"That's not fair, Cinnamon. Your grandmother was never very good in hospitals. It makes her sick."

"So? What better place to be sick if you have to be sick?" I countered.

One thing Daddy wouldn't ever get from me was sympathy for Grandmother Beverly. I never saw her shed a real tear, not even at Grandfather Carlson's funeral, although I have seen her cry at sad scenes in her favorite old movies. She has a lock on the television set in the family room, fixing it on her old-time movie channel. She complains incessantly about today's movies, television, music and books, calling it all depraved and claiming the most degenerate minds are responsible.

Occasionally, I would sit and watch an old movie with her. Some of them are very good, like *Rebecca*. I especially liked the scene where the evil housekeeper, Mrs. Danvers, tries to talk the second Mrs. de Winter into jumping to her death. The first time I saw it, I thought she was going to do it. Mrs. Danvers made it sound so inviting, I felt like jumping.

After I saw the movie, I began to think of Grandmother Beverly as our own Mrs. Danvers trying to talk Mommy into jumping off a cliff or at least helping drive her off the cliff of sanity into the bog of madness, where she now resided.

"That's not funny, Cinnamon," Daddy said. "Some people have less tolerance for unpleasant things."

"Grandmother Beverly? Weaker than other women? Please, Daddy," I said.

He blinked and nibbled on his Danish, quickly falling back to his relaxed demeanor. Daddy has a quiet elegance and charm. He is truly a handsome man with rich dark brown hair and the most striking hazel eyes I have seen on any man. He has those long eyelashes, too, and a perfect nose and firm mouth. He's almost square-jawed with high cheek bones and a forehead that's just wide enough to make him look very intelligent. He's an impeccable dresser and never goes any longer than three weeks without having his hair trimmed.

I understood why Mommy once told me he was the most attractive man who had ever looked at her twice. When she did speak about the early romantic days between them, she emphasized his solid, even-tempered sensibility and how she had come to rely on him to keep

40

her from going too far in one direction or another. Whatever happened to that? I wondered. It was almost as if he had abandoned ship.

"Your mother could be here a while," he said. "Or, she could be moved to a more comfortable place, a place that specializes in her problems."

"You mean a nut house?"

"No, a clinic," he corrected sharply.

I looked away. Tears didn't come into my eyes often, but when they did, I held them over my pupils tightly, battling to keep them locked behind my lids. I took deep breaths.

"We've got to be strong," Daddy said. "For her."

I looked at him. He was checking the time and looking toward the doorway.

"I haven't even learned about today's market results. I hopped on the train as quickly as I could," he muttered.

"Where were you, Daddy? Why weren't you in your office? I thought you have to be there to call your clients while the market is open."

"Sometimes, I go to visit a big account," he explained. "It's good politics. I have an assistant who does a good job covering for me."

"How come you didn't leave a telephone number where you could be reached?"

"I just forgot," he said. "I left too quickly."

Lying is an art form, I thought. Good lying, that is. It requires almost the same techniques, skills and energy that good acting requires.

When you tell lies, you step out of yourself for a while. You become another version of yourself and yet, you have to do it so that the listener believes it's still you talking because he or she has come to trust you, have faith in you. I like making up stories, exaggerating, changing the truth a little — or maybe a little more than a little — sometimes just to see how much I can get away with. It's all in how you hold your head, keep your eyes fixed on the listener and how much sincerity you can squeeze into the small places around the lie.

Maybe Daddy was a bad liar in person because he did most of his lying over the phone. He didn't have to be face-to-face with his customers. He could quote statistics, talk in generalities, blame his mistakes on other people, other businesses or agencies than his own. It's much easier to sound convincing when you talk to an ear and not a pair of eyes.

I knew Daddy was lying, but I didn't know why. It never occurred to me what the reason might be. Maybe I was spending a little too much time in my make-believe world.

"We'd better head home," he said. "You've got schoolwork to do, I'm sure, and there is really nothing else we can do here tonight."

"I want to go see her one more time," I said.

"You might only disturb her more."

"I might help her be comfortable in an uncomfortable place," I countered.

I could hold my gaze on Daddy so firmly that

he would be the first to look away. Mommy taught me how to do that. You actually think of something else, but keep your eyes fixed on the subject.

"All right, but make it quick," he said. "I'm going to make a few phone calls."

He left and I went back upstairs. Mommy had been given a sedative to help her sleep, but she was still moaning and turning her head. I took her hand in mine and spoke softly to her.

"Mommy, it's me. Don't you feel a little better now?"

"Baby . . . born too soon," she muttered.

"What?"

"Little Sacha." She opened her eyes and looked up at me. Then she smiled.

"Cinnamon! How is she?" she asked. "What have they told you?"

I shook my head.

Now she believes she has given birth, I thought, but to a premature baby.

"I know she'll be all right. I know it. She's in the prenatal intensive care unit, but premature babies can do fine. You tell me how she's doing, all right? Tell me," she insisted, squeezing my hand tightly.

If I told her the truth, I thought she'd come apart right before my eyes, her hand crumbling in mine like a dry fall leaf.

"She's doing fine, Mommy. She's getting bigger every moment."

She smiled.

"I knew it. I knew she would. How wonderful. How beautiful. She is beautiful, too, isn't she, Cinnamon? As beautiful as you were when you were born. I'm right? Aren't I?" she asked with a desperation that nearly took my breath away.

"Yes, Mommy, she's beautiful."

"I knew she would be. You've got a little sister. How wonderful. Wonderful," she said relaxing, her eyes closing and staying closed. Her breathing became regular. At least she was relaxed and at ease for a while.

See, I told myself, you can lie better than anyone you know.

Sometimes, that comes in very handy.

Maybe you will be a successful actress, after all.

Daddy and I rode back in silence, mine growing out of the soil of sadness and fear. Daddy looked like he was in deep thought, probably worrying about a stock he had recommended today. Lately, I felt that my father was a guest in his own house, and when he looked at me, he was surprised to discover he had a daughter. It's almost as if he thinks he's having a dream. His whole life — my mother and I, all of it — is just a passing illusion. He would blink hard and we would be gone, I thought. I almost wished it were true.

"How's school?" he asked suddenly. It was as if the question had been stored for months in a cupboard in his brain and he had just stumbled upon it.

"School?"

"Yes, how are you doing in your classes these days?"

"Fine, Daddy. I've been on the honor roll every quarter," I reminded him.

"Oh, right, right. Well, that's good, Cinnamon. You want to get yourself into a fine college like my alma mater, NYU. It's important." He looked at me quickly. "I hope this unfortunate situation won't have a detrimental effect on your school grades. I know it can," he said. "You've just got to be strong and take care of business, consider priorities."

"Mommy's wellbeing is my priority," I said dryly. I wanted to add, as it should be yours, but I kept my lips pressed together as if I were afraid my tongue would run off on its own and say all the things I had been thinking for months and months. Thoughts, words, screams, all were stored in my mouth, waiting to pop out like bees whose hive had been disturbed and sting Daddy in places he couldn't reach. That way, he'd wake up to what had been happening all this last year or so since Grandmother Beverly had moved into our home and invaded our lives.

He should have woken the moment we entered the house. Grandmother Beverly had been busy all day, ever since the ambulance had come to take Mommy to the hospital. The first thing I

45

noticed was that Mommy's favorite two works of art, the pictures she had bought in New Orleans when she and Daddy and I had gone there for a short vacation, were gone from the wall in the hallway. They were both watercolors of swamps with the Spanish moss draping from the trees. In one a toothpick-legged Cajun home was depicted in great detail, shrimp drying on a rock, animal skins hung over a porch railing, and a woman working on the porch weaving a rug. In the other picture, a young couple were in a canoe, poling into the mist. They looked romantic, but in a deeply sad way.

Grandmother Beverly always complained that the pictures were too depressing to be art. She said they were more like someone's nightmares and certainly not the first thing with which to greet a visitor to our home.

"Where are Mommy's pictures?" I demanded as soon as Grandmother Beverly stepped out of the family room.

"How is she now?" she asked my father instead of responding to me.

He shook his head.

"They've given her a sedative, but the doctor wants to treat her for deep depression. If she doesn't snap out of it soon, he's recommending more serious therapy, the sort that takes place in a mental clinic," he replied.

"Exactly what I expected would happen someday. You had to be blind not to see this coming, Taylor."

46

My father didn't agree or disagree. He kept his head slightly bowed, looking like an ashamed young boy confronting his mother.

"Where are Mommy's pictures?" I repeated. She finally turned to me.

"I thought there was enough gloom and doom in this house today. I'm trying to cheer things up."

"Mommy wants those pictures on the wall," I cried. I looked at Daddy. "Make her put them back."

"We'll put up something more pleasant," Grandmother Beverly continued. "I'll buy brighter pictures. We've got to lighten up this hallway. It needs stronger lighting, the walls should be painted a lighter color and I think this entryway rug is worn to a thread. Good riddance to it."

"It is not. What are you talking about? Daddy!" I moaned. "Tell her!"

"I'm so tired," he said. "It's all been quite a shock and right after losing the baby." He shook his head.

"Of course. You're exhausted, Taylor. Come have a nice cup of tea. I made your favorite bis-cuits," she added, "and there's some of that jam you love, the kind that tastes homemade. I bought it for you yesterday."

"Yes, that would be good," he said. He glanced at me. "Don't worry about this stuff now, Cinnamon. It's not what's important at the moment."

47

Grandmother Beverly smiled at me.

"Would you like something, dear?"

Mommy hated her in the kitchen. Until she had suffered the miscarriage, Mommy had not permitted her to make a single dinner for us, even though she claimed she knew all of Daddy's favorite meals. I knew Mommy's resistance wasn't born out of any great desire to be a cook. She warned me from the start that Grandmother Beverly wasn't just moving into the house.

"That woman can't live in a home without taking over," Mommy assured me. "It's not in her nature to be second in any sense. She'll take over and replace me everywhere except in bed, and sometimes," Mommy said her eyes small, "I even fear that."

Of course, she was exaggerating.

That's what I tell myself even though it gave me a different kind of nightmare.

"I'm not hungry," I told Grandmother Beverly, glared furiously once more at Daddy and ran up the stairs to my room, slamming the door behind me.

I was fuming so hot and heavy, I was sure smoke was pouring out of my ears.

The ringing of my phone snapped me out of my seething rage. I took a deep breath and lifted the receiver.

"Hello."

"Cinnamon, what happened?" Clarence asked.

"My mother had to be taken to the hospital," I replied. He was the only one who knew Mommy had suffered a miscarriage. "She's had a nervous breakdown because of what happened."

"Oh, I'm sorry," he said. "Is there anything I can do for you?"

"Yes, call the Mafia and get a hit man over here pronto to save me from my grandmother," I replied.

He laughed, but the sort of short laugh that indicated he knew it really wasn't funny.

"You were all the buzz at school."

"I'm glad the airheads had something to talk about."

"I could see Miss Hamilton was upset for you. You coming to school tomorrow?"

"I'm not staying here, that's for sure," I said.

"What are you going to tell people?" he asked.

"I'll come up with something."

"Let me know so I can be part of it," he said. I knew what he meant. He and I enjoyed making up stories and telling them together, verifying what the other had said, shocking other students whenever we could.

"Meet me at my locker in the morning before homeroom," I told him. He promised he would and hung up.

I fell back spread-eagled on my bed and looked up at the eggshell white ceiling. Sometimes, when I stared into the white void long enough, I'd see the faces of the young women who once lived in this house. It was as if their spirits had been trapped in the walls and I was the only one with whom they could communicate.

My memories of Mommy and me up in the attic returned. They brought tears to my eyes. I wondered if even now, sedated in that hospital room, she was afraid or just sad. Deep inside herself, despite her temporary madness, she must know she has had the miscarriage. Can you get so you could really lie to yourself as well as you could lie to others, actually believing your own fabrications? And is that madness or is it the simplest way to escape the turmoil and unhappiness that sometimes storms around you?

I need inspiration, I thought. I would die before telling anyone the truth. There was only one place to go for it. While Daddy sat below in the kitchen, numbly watching Grandmother Beverly weave a web of control around him, I went up to the attic to conspire with my spirits and my own resourceful imagination.

Mommy told me that when I was only four, I had an imaginary friend. I don't remember, but I've learned it is a very common thing for a child to do: create his or her own companion. Maybe it's just as hard to be alone when you're very young as it is to be alone when you're very old, I thought. Old people imagine friends, too.

There's something about growing up, about

being in society and mixing with real people that restricts your imaginative powers. If you say something that seems like fantasy, people laugh at you or make you feel self-conscious about it, so you smother your make-believe and drive the creative thoughts down into the grave, bury them in the cemetery of originality, and work harder at being like everyone else, safe, unremarkable, just some more wallpaper. It takes courage to revive your imagination and risk the ridicule. In an ironic sense, it takes a brave soul to contrive exaggerations, fantasies, elaborate and eloquent lies.

I flipped the switch and the dark attic became illuminated, but not so brightly as to drive away the small shadows and brighten the dark corners. Neither Mommy nor I wanted it that well lit anyway. Some darkness is comforting, warm, inviting. Mommy used to say it felt protective.

"Most people are afraid of the dark," she said. "They'll never trespass on our privacy."

There was some old furniture up here, dusty and worn. If Grandmother Beverly ever made the trek up the second set of narrow stairs and opened the attic door, she would gasp and vow instantly to have it immediately cleaned out. None of it had any real value anymore. That was true, but there were other kinds of value than monetary value. For Mommy and me this small, dusty room had always been cozy, inviting, comfortable.

Dust particles spun in the beam of the light, glistening like particles of diamonds. It had been a while since Mommy and I were up here. When we were coming up here more frequently, we did do some cleaning, washing down the two windows and sills, vacuuming and some polishing. We wanted it to maintain its special charm, but we wanted it to be clean enough to inhabit as well.

If there were rodents up here, they were excellent at keeping themselves invisible. We never found any droppings and the worst thing we did discover were spiders. Mommy thought we should leave some of the webs untouched. They weren't poisonous spiders. She called them nature's housekeepers who kept any other insects in check.

There were some areas of dampness, places where rain had seeped through or in between cracks. We would burn incense to drive away any musty odors or sometimes spray some flower-scented air freshener.

I went directly to our incense burner and lit a stick. Then I opened the window so the tiny smoke would spiral in that direction.

Mommy and I always felt the attic had been someone's hideaway at one time or another. On the floor there had been a brown oval rug, worn through in many spots and very faded; why would anyone have put a rug up here if it wasn't a place for some sort of retreat or privacy.

"Maybe the children used it as a playhouse," Mommy suggested, "or maybe Carolyne Demerest had a lover and brought him up here for romantic trysts," she pondered, her eyes widening with excitement.

We both decided that was more fun and elaborated on the story.

Carolyne Demerest had fallen in love with the young groundskeeper.

"Who was a closet poet, leaving the poems tacked to a special tree."

"And she fell in love with him through his words!"

"Just like Elizabeth and Robert Browning," I added.

"Exactly, and the first time they met up here . . ."

"It was snowing. The window was glazed and she sat in this old rocker wrapped in a heavy shawl she had made herself."

"He fell to her feet and held them against his cheeks and said . . ."

"I have dreamed all my life of this moment."

We both laughed and laughed. What fun it was. I could almost hear her laughter now and feel her hugging me. We were like sisters, truly. I was the sister she had wanted, and her daughter and best friend forever and ever.

Mommy, I cried looking at the empty rocking chair.

I sat there on the small settee and wondered what she was dreaming in her deep sleep, what were the images and the words. What could hold her so firmly and keep her from wanting to see and be with me so much that she couldn't overcome her mental problems?

Surely, I'll wake up tomorrow morning to the sound of commotion, lots of footsteps, doors opening and closing, a car horn and some cries of delight. I'll rise from my bed and look down at our driveway where I will see a car stop and Mommy step out, looking like her old self, strong, full of energy, joyous at the sight of her beloved old home. She would be cured and the first words out of her lips would be, "Where's Cinnamon? Where's my little girl?"

Mommy, I would cry inside, Mommy.

And I would practically fly out of my room, descending the stairway so quickly that I couldn't remember my feet touching a step, and then I'd go charging out the front door and into her awaiting arms.

She would hold me and kiss me and say, "Don't worry, sweetheart. I'm back.

"All will be well again," she would promise.

She and I would enter the house and she would look up at the wall and demand to know where her two works of art were.

"Who dared take them off the wall?"

Daddy would hurry to the basement — or wherever they had been hidden — and he would rush to get them up.

"Sorry," he would say. "I just wasn't paying attention to these things."

"Well, now that I'm home, see that you do," Mommy would tell him.

And Grandmother Beverly would pop like a bubble and be gone along with all the other demons that haunted our home.

We could change the channel on the television set. We could play our music and light our candles and talk to the lonely dead spirits.

And never be afraid of the darkness.

3

Playing the Part

I fell asleep in my chair, dreaming about the love story Mommy and I had created in the attic. It wasn't what I had intended to do, but it almost didn't matter that I didn't come up with a story to tell the Nosy Parkers in school. I decided to simply ignore their curiosity and hope they would stop gaping at me, but Grandmother Beverly was right about gossip, especially about gossip concerning us. It had its own life, its own momentum. People act like they don't want anything to do with you, but as soon as they can learn something about you, they seize it and then take great pleasure in spreading the news, especially if it's bad news. It didn't take too long, less than forty-eight hours, actually.

Classes at my school might as well have been interrupted and an announcement delivered over the public-address system that went something like, "Attention, attention. Two days ago Cinnamon Carlson's mother had a mental breakdown."

That was how fast the news about my family spread. Reactions of my teachers went from aloofness to pity to looks that said, "It's not surprising to me."

The only teacher who did show sympathy and concern was Miss Hamilton. When the bell rang to end class, she asked me to stay a moment. She waited for the rest of the class to leave and then she turned to me, giving me her best long face and saddest eyes and asked how I was doing.

"I'm fine," I told her.

"I want you to know you can come to me anytime, Cinnamon. Please don't hesitate," she said as if we both suffered from the same disease. Well, she lived alone and, these days, I felt alone; maybe loneliness is a disease, but everyone has his or her own way of curing it, I thought. If she knew some of the things I did, like talk to the dead Carolyne and her son Abraham at their grave sites, she might not be so anxious to have me try out for one of her plays.

I nodded, kept my eyes down, and left as quickly as I could. Clarence was waiting for me in the hallway.

"What was that all about?"

"Act One, Scene Two," I said.

"What?"

"Nothing. Forget it. I'm hungry," I said and marched off to the cafeteria.

Clarence had to sit near a window and preferably one on his left side. If there wasn't a seat free that satisfied him, he would eat outside at the bench tables we used in the early fall or spring, no matter how cold it was. Fortunately, today, a day with a dreary overcast sky and a constant northerly wind, there were free seats at a table right below a window. He rushed to it and put down his books to claim the place. I followed and put my books beside his before going into the lunch line.

Sometimes, I brought my lunch, which usually consisted of a container of yogurt and an apple, but with all the commotion at home, I had not had time to buy any yogurt and Grandmother Beverly certainly hadn't bought any for me. She didn't consider it to be proper food. She called it novelty food or, if anything, a dessert. It did no good to read the description of nutrients on the side of the cup.

Today, I thought I would just have some soup and a platter of chicken salad. When I glanced to the right, I saw the heads of other students practically touching temple to temple as they gazed my way and cackled. In moments, I expected to see eggs rolling under the table.

I got my food as quickly as I could and returned to our table. No one else had sat there yet.

"So, they moved her?" Clarence asked as he started on his platter of macaroni and cheese, eating from the left side of the plate.

"This morning," I replied. "I'm going to visit her right after school."

"Your father, too?"

"No. He'll be there at night after his dinner meeting in the city, or so he says."

"Don't you believe him?" Clarence asked, surprised at my tone of voice.

I was silent, thinking about the last two days. Mommy's illness had rejuvenated Grandmother Beverly. She now had the strength and stamina of a forty-year-old. The morning following Mommy's being taken to the hospital, Grandmother Beverly was up ahead of Daddy. I heard her moving about the hallway and down the stairs.

Because Daddy was a broker on Wall Street, he had to be out of the house very early to make his commute and be ready for the opening bell at the stock market. I never saw him at breakfast during the week, but up until the last year or so, Mommy would get up to be with him. Grandmother Beverly sometimes didn't rise until I was about to leave for school, and she never rose early enough to say good-bye to Daddy in the morning.

Suddenly, she was doing it.

By the time I was dressed and down to breakfast, Daddy was already gone, of course; but Grandmother Beverly was still in the kitchen. I heard the dishes clanking as well as pots and pans. Curiosity quickened my footsteps. I stopped in the doorway and what I saw shocked and confused me.

"What are you doing?" I asked her.

She had taken all of the dishes out of the

kitchen cabinets, and the pots and pans as well, and was reorganizing everything.

"This kitchen was never set up intelligently," she replied. "Cups and dishes and soup bowls all scattered about in different cabinets, and the pots and pans . . . why are they under the salad sink? They should be nearer the stove. You know how hard it was to find a can opener in this kitchen? Just ridiculous to have all this chaos."

"Mommy never has any trouble finding what she wants. She's going to be very upset when she gets home," I said.

"She'll get over it quickly, especially when she realizes how well organized it is now. If she gets home," she added in a mutter so low, I barely heard it.

"You can't do this," I insisted. "Put it all back where it was."

"Don't be silly, Cinnamon. Now get some decent breakfast in you and go to school," she ordered. "What do you have, eggs, cold cereal?"

"Does Daddy know you've done this?"

She turned and raised her eyebrows.

"You think I need my son to tell me what's right and what isn't? But to answer you, yes, he does," she continued and turned back to the cabinets. "Not only are things in the wrong places, but these cabinets need to be relined with cabinet paper. What good is it to wash your dishes and then put them on a dirty shelf?"

"They aren't dirty."

"Oh, you know? When was the last time you did any real housework here? When I was your age, I had to make all the beds and dust the furniture in the living room before I could go to school, even if it meant I'd be late."

"Brilliant," I said.

I turned and marched out of the house.

"Cinnamon!" she called after me. "Where are you going without your breakfast?"

I didn't answer. What she heard instead was the door slamming behind me.

Now, two days later, she had completed her revamping of the kitchen and was working on the living room and preparing our dinners. However, up until now, she had been left to eat them by herself. Daddy was working late and I didn't come home for dinner either night, going directly to the hospital to sit with Mommy. She slept most of the time I was there, and when she awoke, she was full of questions about Sacha and plans for what she would be doing when Sacha was released from the prenatal intensive care unit.

"I just know we'll both be better about the same time," she told me.

I wondered what she thought was supposedly wrong with her, but I was afraid to ask. I was actually afraid to ask her any questions. She would cry often and then say, "It's all right. I'll be fine."

I tried talking about the house, tried to get her interested in coming home quickly.

"Grandmother Beverly is changing things," I said. "You need to get better and come home quickly."

"Is she? That's all right. We'll just change it all back," she told me. For a moment I thought she was returning to her old self, but then she added, "I just can't wait to show her Sacha, to show her what a beautiful new granddaughter she has, a granddaughter she never wanted. How sorry she will be for the things she's said. Won't she be, Cinnamon?"

"Yes," I said weakly.

As long as Mommy was like this, Grandmother Beverly felt the power that comes with being right, predicting accurately and then never letting us forget it. She was practically beating Daddy over the head with this tragedy daily, shoving his face in the reality, washing out his mouth with her soap of truth.

The first two nights, he came to the hospital directly from work, looking fatigued, defeated. The market happened to be down, too, and that was depressing him. Some of his best clients were blaming him for his recommendations, he said.

"When they make money, I'm a hero. When they lose, I'm an idiot."

"Why did you ever want to be a broker, Daddy?" I asked while he and I sat at Mommy's bedside watching her drift in and out of sleep.

He shrugged.

"Money always excited me. There's nothing more beautiful than watching a small investment become bigger and bigger and then knowing when to sell. There's all that suspense. Right there in front of me events are transpiring that will affect people's lives, lose or make their jobs, destroy their retirement pensions or turn them into wealthy people. I like being part of that. I feel . . . plugged into the current that runs the country. Does that make sense?" he asked almost wistfully.

"I guess so," I said.

Actually, I had never heard him speak so passionately about his work before and for a few moments, I was actually mesmerized. Most of the time, he moved about so methodically, thinking and acting with a surgeon's care — analyzing, scrutinizing every little thing, right down to the portion of soap powder it took to wash floors. I was beginning to wonder if he was emotionally dead, if he cried or laughed or cared warmly about anything, especially Mommy and me.

"Are you upset about losing the baby?" I asked.

"Sure," he said. "But . . ."

"But what, Daddy? Don't say Grandmother Beverly might have been right. Don't dare say that," I warned him.

"No. Not exactly. I just wonder if Amber would have been strong enough for it, for raising a child from infancy again. She seemed so fragile, I began to wonder if we had done the right thing. Not because of her age," he quickly added. "I just wonder if she had the temperament for it."

"She had it. She would have been a wonderful mother to a new baby," I insisted.

He nodded, but not with any confidence. He simply nodded to shut me up.

We were both quiet then, both lost in our own thoughts, almost strangers on a train who just happened to be seated side by side. I had no idea where this train was heading.

All these events and discussions passed through my mind when Clarence asked me if I believed my father when he told me he would visit Mommy at the mental hospital after his dinner meeting.

"No," I finally replied. "I don't believe things he tells me these days. Lately, I keep finding his lies scattered all around the house."

"Huh?"

"Never mind," I said. "I have other things on my mind at the moment."

After school I got into my car and headed for the Chester Alton Psychiatric Hospital, a privately run institution outside of Yonkers where Mommy had been placed that morning. It was just far enough to be a good long ride. The car was really Mommy's car, but even before she had become pregnant and had her aches and pains, she had hardly used it. I already had logged twice as many miles on it than she had.

It wasn't just hard to believe I was on my way to visit my mother in a mental clinic; it was painful and actually very frightening. I could feel the trembling start in my legs and slowly vibrate up into my spine as I drew closer and closer to the clinic.

When I parked and got out, the building looked intimidating. It was so white that with the afternoon sun slipping out from under clouds, the reflection made me reach for my sunglasses. The moment I saw my image in the car window, a whole new persona came over me and helped me face what I had to do: visit my mother in a mental hospital. It was just too difficult to do it as her daughter.

I brushed back my hair, took a deep breath and moved forward like an actress about to step on a stage. It felt good, liberating. I walked differently, held my head differently and stepped up to the front entrance. Pretending was like wearing a mask and when I wore a mask, no one could see how terrible and how frightened I felt inside.

The lobby was deceiving. It wasn't that it was too immaculate — the tile floor gleaming, the furniture looking brand new. It was too cozy, too warm. I was expecting almost as much security as a prison with bars on all the windows and patients wandering about in house gowns, babbling or just staring vacantly at their own empty minds and sterile walls.

However, these walls had many pretty pictures, oils of pleasant country scenes, people with happy faces, bright flowers. There were fresh flowers in vases on tables and magazines neatly organized in a rack on the right wall. On the left was a small area with a television set. Three people sat on a sofa, all nicely dressed. I had the sense that one of them might be a patient, but there was no way to tell who were the visitors and who was the patient. Maybe they were all patients.

I thought the place resembled an upscale hotel lobby more than it did a psychiatric clinic.

A pretty young nurse sat behind a reception counter. She looked up and smiled at me as I approached.

"May I help you?" she asked. For some reason she reminded me of my dentist's assistant, her teeth glittering through that Colgate smile. I was almost expecting her to follow with, "Do you floss?"

"Yes," I said. "I'm here to see Amber Carlson."

"Amber Carlson?" She looked down at a large book and turned the page, reading. "Immediate family only," she muttered.

"I'm her younger sister," I said. "I've just flown in from Los Angeles and driven here directly from the airport."

"Oh."

"How is she?"

"Well, I don't have updates as to patients' conditions, but let me call the nurse's station and advise them of your arrival."

"Thank you." I gazed around as she dialed and informed the head nurse. She listened a moment and then thanked her and hung up.

"Mrs. Mendelson asked if you could please give them a few minutes. Your sister has just had a therapeutic bath and they're getting her back to bed," she said.

"Oh, fine."

"Los Angeles. How was your trip?"

"Smooth," I said. "I had forgotten how beautiful the foliage is here in the fall. Living in southern California," I said "you just forget the dramatic changes of season."

"Oh. What do you do in Los Angeles?"

"I work for a television production company. I'm a P.A."

"P.A.?"

"Production assistant. It's a way to get yourself into the business."

"What do you want to be?"

"An actress," I said as if it was the dumbest question she could ask.

"Oh, of course. You're pretty enough to be an actress. I bet you're good."

"I hope I am," I said. "My grandmother has such faith in me. She's the one who sends me enough money to keep trying. You don't make all that much money as a P.A., and it's so expensive to live out there. You need someone to be your patron, to support and believe in you."

"I bet."

"I auditioned for the part of a nurse recently," I said. "For a soap opera."

"Really? Which one?" she asked excitedly. "I follow one religiously."

"It's a new one, just starting. It's called *Transfusions*."

"*Transfusions*?"

"It's set in a hospital."

"Oh, right."

"I don't know if it will get on the air, but I tried out anyway. I'll hear next week. It's very nerve-racking."

"I bet," she said nodding.

"I was very upset when I heard about my sister. I know she wanted that baby very much. It doesn't surprise me that she's had this reaction to the disaster."

I held my breath, waiting for her to tell me that what happened to my mother was not all that unusual.

"I'm sure she'll get well soon," she said with little emotion. She obviously didn't know my mother's condition. The phone rang. She said hello and then nodded at me. "Take the elevator to the fifth floor and turn left. She's in the first room on your left," she instructed.

"Thank you."

I took out my compact mirror and glanced at myself. It seemed to me that would be a thing my mother's actress sister would do. When I looked at the receptionist, she smiled and nodded. I smiled back and sauntered over to the elevator.

When I stepped out of it on the fifth floor and turned left, I saw a nurse come around the desk and approach me quickly.

"I'm Mrs. Mendelson," she said. "She's still somewhat medicated, but I'm sure she'll be happy to see a familiar face."

"Thank you," I said. "I won't stay too long this first visit. Jet lag," I added.

She smiled.

"I understand."

She escorted me down to the room and paused at the door.

"She's still confused, suffering from traumatic amnesia. It's best you don't directly confront anything she says for the moment. She's like a patient with an open wound, but don't worry, she'll soon emerge from this and be fine."

"Thank you," I said and I entered.

Mommy was lying with her eyes open, her head supported by a large white pillow. She seemed smaller, paler to me. It brought tears to my eyes.

There were flowers in a vase on the stand beside her bed. I thought Daddy had sent them, but I looked and saw there was no card. It was probably just something the hospital did.

Mommy looked at me as if she didn't recognize me for a moment and I wondered if I had done such a good job of changing my personality that even my mother was confused. Then she smiled.

"Cinnamon," she said reaching up for me.

"Hi, Mommy," I said. I quickly kissed her and pulled the chair closer to the bed. "How are you feeling now?"

"Very tired," she said. "Have you seen Sacha today?" she asked without taking a breath.

"No. I just came from school, Mommy."

"Oh, right. I've lost track of time." She smiled. "I don't even know what day it is. What day is it?"

"It's Thursday, Mommy."

"Good, good. That's how many days now?" Her eyes blinked rapidly. "How many since her birth, Cinnamon? Three, four?"

"Three," I said.

"Three. Good. Every new day brings more hope. We've got to worry for a while, but she'll be fine, won't she?"

"Yes, Mommy, she'll be fine."

"Good." She closed her eyes. And then she opened them abruptly. "I want your father to get one of those baby monitors . . . you know, where you can hear if the baby cries? Of course, I'll have her sleep right beside us when we take her home, but even after she's out of danger, older, I want to have that. Too many babies die of crib death or choke on something. When you're that small and fragile . . .

70

it's just a good idea, isn't it?"

"Yes," I said.

"Remind him, remind your father. He's so forgetful these days."

As if talking about him brought him to life, he called. I picked up the phone.

"Cinnamon. I'm glad you're there already. How's she doing?" he asked.

"The same," I said.

"Right. Don't worry though. The doctor assures me she's going to make a full recovery."

"What time are you arriving, Daddy?"

"I'm not sure at the moment. I just found out I've got to go to Brooklyn for this meeting. I was under the impression it was here in Manhattan. That's going to add at least an hour to my travel time."

"Can't you get out of it?"

"It's pretty important. Heavy hitters," he added.

"Mommy's been hit pretty heavy," I responded. He was silent a moment.

"She doesn't even remember if I'm there or not at the moment, Cinnamon."

"That doesn't matter. You'll remember you were here," I said sharply.

"Okay. Let me speak to her. Let's see what she says to me," he said and I handed Mommy the phone.

"It's Daddy," I said.

"Hello, Taylor?"

She listened.

"I need you to get something," she said and then she put the phone aside and looked at me. "What do I need? I forget."

"I'll tell him later, Mommy. Don't worry."

"Oh. Good. It's all right, Taylor. Cinnamon knows and will tell you. Is everything all right?"

She listened and nodded as if she thought he could see her through the wire, and then she handed me the phone.

"Hello?"

"I'll try to get there," he promised me.

"Whatever," I said.

"How are you doing?"

"I'm terrific. Matter of fact, Daddy, I think I'm going to win the Academy Award this year for the best all-around performance as a loving granddaughter. She was rearranging the living room when I left this morning. The bathrooms might be next, if she can pull up the toilets and tubs."

"All right, all right," he said in a tired voice. "I'll have a talk with her this week. I promise."

"You know what promises are, Daddy? Lies with pretty ribbons tied on them. I'll see you later," I added quickly and hung up.

Mommy stared at me and for a long moment, I thought she realized what was really happening and was coming out of it, crawling up from the dark pit of her temporary madness into the light of day like a restored heroine about to do battle with all the forces of evil. We'd be a team again.

Then she smiled that strange, distant smile.

"You know what I want you to do?" she asked. I shook my head. "I want you to sneak a camera into the prenatal intensive care unit and take Sacha's picture for me. Bring it here next time, okay. Will you?"

I took a deep breath to keep my throat from completely closing and nodded.

"Good," she said. "Good." She closed her eyes again. I reached for her hand and held it and sat there for nearly half an hour, waiting for her to open her eyes again.

She didn't and when the nurse looked in, I rose and smiling at her told her I was tired, too. I'd be back tomorrow.

"She'll get better in a matter of days," she promised.

Another lie wrapped in a pretty ribbon, I thought and went to the elevator.

There was a different receptionist behind the desk in the lobby when I stepped out. She looked up at me, but I didn't feel like performing anymore.

I hurried out and to the car where I sat for a while, catching my breath. I dreaded going home, not only because of what else I might find my grandmother had changed but because Mommy's absence, the heavy silence in light of where she now was, would be hard to face. Instead, on the way, I stopped at a pizza place and bought myself a couple of slices. I sat in a quiet corner and ate them watching some younger kids talk animatedly, a pretty girl of about fourteen at the center, wearing head-phones and listening to a portable CD player while the boys vied for her attention.

I envied their innocence, their wide-eyed fas-cination with everything they saw, touched and did. How had I grown so old so fast? I won-dered.

After I ate, I decided to call Clarence. I needed to talk to someone.

He came out of his house to meet me in my car when I drove up. I told him what I had done when I arrived at the psychiatric hospital.

"And she believed you? You're so much younger than your mother," he remarked.

"She never doubted it."

He laughed.

"I guess you are good."

"It helped me go in and up to my mother's room, but it didn't do me any good when I was with her. There are some things you can't pre-tend away," I told him.

He nodded.

"What about your father?"

I described the conversation.

"Maybe he just had to go to the meeting," he said.

"Maybe. Would you?" I quickly asked.

"I don't know. I guess I would try to get out of it. People should understand why and excuse him."

"Exactly," I said.

"Well, what are you going to do?"

"I don't know," I said.

"Miss Hamilton pulled me aside at the end of the day today. I was on my way out of the building. She wanted to talk about you. She said, 'I know you and Cinnamon are close friends.' "

He looked at me.

"I guess we are," he said.

"Of course we are — so? What did she want? To tell you how she'll be there for me or something?"

"No, she wanted me to try to talk you into going out for the play. She said you'd need something like being in a play more now."

"I'm already in a play," I said.

"What? Where?"

"At home. It's called, *A Happy Family*," I said.

Clarence laughed.

I started the engine.

"I'd better get home," I said. "I haven't even begun any homework yet and who knows? Grandmother Beverly might have moved my room into the pantry or something by now."

He shook his head and opened the door. For a moment he just looked at me as if he were making a big decision. Then he leaned over and kissed me on the left cheek.

"Good night," he said quickly.

I touched my cheek.

75

Even that, I thought, even a kiss was a ritual for him and had to be done from left to right.

I laughed.

It was the only laugh I had had all day.

4

A Father's Lies

Grandmother had concentrated her efforts on Daddy's office this day. I didn't know how she had done it, but all by herself she had moved his heavy dark oak desk across the room so it faced the window on the east side, and once she had done that, she had to change everything: lamps, chairs, the small sofa, tables and even rearrange books.

"Why didn't you come home for dinner?" she demanded as soon as I entered the house. She had been watching one of her movies and keeping one ear turned to hear me or Daddy come home. The second I closed the door, she was in the hallway.

"I went directly to the hospital and visited with Mommy," I told her.

"You were there all this time?"

"It's not down the street," I replied without much emotion. "Don't you want to know how she is?"

"I've already spoken to your father about her," she told me.

"Really? Well considering he wasn't there, I'm sure he was very informative."

"He's been in contact with her doctor, which is more important," she insisted.

"Is it? You think that's more important than having your husband come see you, be with you, comfort you?"

"Don't start with your dramatics," she warned. "All of you children are so theatrical these days. It comes from spending so much time in front of the television set," she analyzed. "It's either that or staring into a mirror all day."

"I don't do either, Grandmother, and you know that. Matter of fact, you watch more television than I do, and you wear more makeup," I added.

"Don't be insolent."

"I'm not being insolent. I'm just stating facts."

"Never mind, never mind," she insisted. "There are far more important things to talk about and do. I'm getting this house intelligently organized. Come see your father's study," she told me.

It was really more of a command, but I was too curious not to follow her, and when I saw it, I smiled to myself.

If he doesn't like it, too bad, I thought.

"He works mainly in the afternoon when he works here on the weekends. He shouldn't be facing the sunlight. Don't you agree?"

"Fine with me," I said. Then I looked at her, my eyes small, determined. "Don't come into my room, Grandmother. If you move so much as a picture frame on the dresser . . ."

"I have no intention of entering your cave," she said. "You'll have to repair your room yourself."

"It doesn't need repairing. It needs to be left alone," I told her.

"Have you done your homework?" she cried after me when I turned away and started for the stairs.

I paused and looked at her, a half-smile on my face.

"Have I done my homework? Since when have you ever asked about that?"

"Well, with your mother gone, I thought I had better —"

"My mother isn't gone!" I screamed at her. "She's just recuperating. At least she's able to recuperate from her madness, which is more than some people can do."

I charged up the stairs, anxious to get away from her. She simply returned to her old movie, wallowing in it like she would soak in a warm bath.

It took me hours to calm myself down and do my homework. It was nearly midnight when I went to bed and still, Daddy had not come home. I fell asleep, but I woke to the sound of his footsteps on the stairs. Those stairs always creaked loudly, which was part of the charm of the house for me and for Mommy. Daddy didn't like it and Grandmother Beverly thought they should be ripped out and redone. She said the house was too old to be inhabited and complained vehemently about the creaks in the walls, the moans in the pipes, and the leaks in the roof. I would smile to myself, imagining her awake at night listening to the sounds, terrified that the house itself was coming alive and closing in on her. Footsteps on the stairway echoed with electric speed over the hallway floor and into her room as well as my own, but she didn't get up to greet Daddy.

I rose quickly and went to my door just as Daddy was passing my room.

"Daddy," I called in a loud whisper. He had his shoulders slumped like someone trying to tiptoe guiltily away.

"What are you doing awake?" he asked.

"I heard you coming up. Did you get to see Mommy?"

He shook his head.

"It was a horrendous trip. There were accidents and delays and I just managed to get home now. I'll get there tomorrow," he said, "but I did call and the nurse told me she was resting comfortably."

"She's drugged. How would they know if she was comfortable, Daddy?"

"All right," he said. "It's late, Cinnamon. Let's talk about it all tomorrow."

"When?"

"When I see you," he said. "Go to sleep. You're just going to make things more difficult

80

for everyone by being contentious," he added and walked on to his bedroom.

I stood there and watched him go in, closing the door softly behind him.

He's not the same, I thought. He's just not the same. There's something more than Mommy's condition affecting him. I knew he would never tell me what it was. Could it be he was in trouble financially? Were we on the brink of economic disaster? Did he depend on Grandmother's money these days? Was that why he wouldn't contest anything she did?

Falling asleep with these questions in the air was like trying to walk over an icy road. Every time I drew close to drifting off, another troubling thought jerked me back awake, keeping me slipping and sliding until I finally passed out just before dawn. I hadn't set the alarm and my grandmother actually had to come pounding on my door.

"Are you getting up or not?" she cried from the hallway. I heard her try the knob, but I had locked it. "Who locks their bedroom?" she muttered. She knocked again. "Cinnamon, are you getting up?"

I groaned and looked at the clock, astounded at the time myself. For a moment I considered not going to school at all, and then, all my questions from the night before began to flood over me again and I made a quick decision. I was up and dressed in minutes.

"Why do you lock your bedroom door?"

Grandmother Beverly asked as soon as I stepped into the kitchen. I went right to the coffee without responding. She made it too weak for my taste and even for Daddy's, but he didn't complain. I deliberately poured a cup and then poured it back through the coffee maker.

"What are you doing?"

"Trying to turn this tea into coffee," I muttered.

"A girl your age shouldn't be drinking so much coffee. It's not good for you," she insisted.

I started to look for one of my breakfast bars. She had moved everything around in the cabinets and literally nothing, not even a salt shaker, was where it had been. I started to shove things to the side more frantically.

"You're messing it all up. What are you looking for? Just ask," she said.

I turned.

"My breakfast bars! Where are they?"

"Oh, that garbage. It's candy. How can that be breakfast? I threw it all out," she admitted, proudly.

"Threw it all out? I had just bought them. They were mine. You had no right to do that, Grandmother, and for your information, they have a great deal more nutritional value than what you and Daddy eat for breakfast."

"Nonsense. Don't believe what they write on those wrappers," she said. "Now I'll make you some hard-boiled eggs." She put the pot under the faucet.

I gulped some coffee and marched past her.

"Cinnamon," she called after me. "Where are you going?"

"I'm too late to eat breakfast," I shouted back. "You eat it for me."

I rushed out of the house and to my car. My wheels screamed and stained the driveway with rubber as I accelerated. I was sure she had heard it. When I got to the road, I didn't head directly for school. Instead, I swung around toward Clarence's house and sure enough, I caught him sauntering along. He lived only about a half-mile from the school in the most elegant and expensive area. His house was actually as big as mine. He was surprised when I pulled up and honked the horn.

"What's up?" he asked after he opened the passenger door.

"I'm not going to school today," I said.

"Oh?"

"I have something else to do. Want to come along?"

"Where?"

"Into the city," I said. "Manhattan."

He thought a moment and then looked back as if someone was watching us. He shrugged and got into the car.

"I guess," he said.

I shot away from the curb and headed for the thruway.

"So what do you have to do?" he asked. "And don't say shopping. I hate shopping. If it's shopping, let me out. My mother used to drag me like a sled through the department stores."

"Hardly shopping. I'm going into the city to spy on my father," I replied.

"What? Why?"

"I have a feeling he might be losing his job or something," I said. "He might even have lost it by now. He's been acting strange and it's not because of what's happened to my mother. He's a bundle of secrets, wound up tight, and he won't let me inside. Sometimes, I feel like I don't care anymore, but then I think I should."

"Of course, you should," Clarence agreed. "Who else is going to care if you don't?"

From what he had told me about his own family life, he didn't have a much better relationship with his father who was a very busy attorney specializing in estate planning. His mother managed the new mall north of Yonkers and, according to Clarence, was busier than his father. He had a younger sister Lindsey in ninth grade, but they weren't close. Most of the time, they walked right by each other in school, barely exchanging a glance. He said she was very spoiled.

Funny, I thought, how you could be so alone in your own home, in your own family. Just because you had parents, it didn't guarantee you wouldn't be an orphan or a stranger if your parents were so wrapped up in themselves.

Sometimes, I thought Clarence hung around with me and listened to my moans and groans just so he could feel like he was in a real family, even though it was mine and not his own.

"How are you going to spy on him?"

"I know where he works. We'll hang out there," I explained.

"Doesn't sound like you have much of a plan."

"I've got to do it. If you don't want to come . . ."

"No, it's all right. I'm fine."

It wasn't until we reached the Wall Street area that I felt I might have made a very silly decision. The traffic, the crowds and just the size of the buildings made what I had planned to do look as foolish as Clarence had made it sound.

"What do we do first?" Clarence asked, even more impressed with the task himself now.

"Find a parking garage as close to Daddy's building as possible," I said. I tried to look and sound like I knew what I was doing, like I was in the city often, but of course I wasn't. Mommy didn't like going to the city, except to shows. I saw my first Broadway show with her and Daddy when I was only seven. It was a musical, *The Phantom of the Opera*, and I remember being so mesmerized and excited, I could hardly speak.

"That's where you'll belong someday, Cinnamon," Mommy whispered in my ear and nodded at the stage.

I wondered. Did I? Could I?

I saw a few shows a year after that, but most of the time recently, it was just Mommy and me. Daddy was either working or meeting clients.

Parking was the easiest part of my skimpy plan today. It just meant spending money, which we did, and then we walked to Daddy's building.

"Have you ever been here before?" Clarence asked.

"Once, a long time ago. We had a day off but the market was open and Daddy decided to take me to see his offices and all the activity. I was in the fifth grade. Mommy came along and afterward, she and I went to a show off-Broadway, *The Fantasticks*. It was a very exciting day.

"I thought Daddy had a mad, crazy job. All that shouting and excitement. I couldn't understand how anyone kept track of anything or knew what he or she was doing. Daddy looked like the calmest person there."

Clarence listened, intrigued. He wasn't in the city that often, so his eyes were wandering everywhere, drinking in the activity, the endless flow of people, cars, the billboards and the variety of stores and restaurants. I wondered if your brain could shut down like some overloaded computer, all these sights and sounds coming at you at once.

"Now what?" he asked.

"There's a coffee shop in his building, in the lobby. Let's go there."

We went in and were able to get a table close to the window that looked out at the lobby. Having had nothing for breakfast, I was hungry and ordered scrambled eggs and a bagel. Clarence just had some coffee and watched me eat. I watched the elevators. There were four, with a constant stream of traffic, but soon it started to taper off. Most people had already arrived for work.

"What exactly do you think your father's doing?" Clarence asked as I ate.

"I think he's looking for a new job. That's why he doesn't tell his secretary exactly where he's going or where he can be reached or why he didn't answer a page the other day."

Clarence nodded.

"Yeah, that makes sense," he said. "He's probably got a lot of pride and doesn't want to feel like some kind of failure. My father has never made a mistake in twenty years of practicing law."

"Really?"

"That's what he makes it sound like, and everyone who works for my mother is a half-wit." He smiled. "I come from a pair of regular geniuses."

He made me laugh. Clarence is handsome, I thought. He has a twinkle in his eye that gets pretty sexy sometimes, whether he knows it or not. He acts like he doesn't, but I was always suspicious of people, especially boys. Their smiles and words were like little balls in the hands of a magician: now you see them, now you don't.

When I finished eating, I paid the check and lingered for a few moments.

"Now what do we do?" he asked.

"I want to be sure he's upstairs at his desk. I'll call and pretend I'm a client and ask for him," I said. "Afterward, we can go to the magazine and newspaper shop and then we'll hang out and wait until the market closes to see what he does. We've just got to keep inconspicuous."

We went to the bank of pay phones in the lobby and I dialed Daddy's number. His secretary answered and I asked for him.

"Oh," she said, "he's just this moment left. Can I switch you to Mr. Posner who's handling his accounts in the interim?"

"No," I said and hung up quickly.

"He left," I told Clarence excitedly. "Just now!"

We hurried back to the lobby and went into the newspaper and magazine store, pretending to be looking for something while I kept my eyes on the elevators. Moments later, Daddy emerged. He walked quickly toward the entrance and we shot out after him.

"We've got to be careful. I don't want him to spot us," I said as we stepped out.

Daddy was walking briskly down the sidewalk, his black wool scarf flung over his shoulders. He looked dapper, as dapper and handsome as Cary Grant in one of Grandmother Beverly's favorite old movies.

"I've seen this done enough on television," Clarence said confidently. "Just keep a good distance between us and him and try to stay behind someone."

Daddy never looked back, so it didn't matter. He crossed the street and continued down another busier street. Minutes later, he entered a coffee shop. It wasn't a very large one, but it had two big front windows. We could see everyone in it.

"He's just taking a coffee break," Clarence muttered. "He's not visiting any new firm."

I nodded, but Daddy strolled past the counter and paused at a booth. For a moment, because of the angle we were at, it looked like an empty one, but when he leaned over, we moved to our right and we caught sight of him greeting a woman, a very elegant looking blond-haired woman in a business suit. She seized his hand and held it as he slid into the seat across from her and for a long moment, they just looked at each other. Then Daddy smiled and sat back. She didn't let go of his hand.

I felt as if the air had just leaked completely out of my lungs and was quickly replaced with some steaming hot liquid burning in my chest and up into my mouth. It seemed like minutes flew by and still, they were holding hands.

"Maybe it's just a client," Clarence offered charitably.

My eyes clashed with his hopeful look.

"You don't hold hands with your clients," I managed to reply.

We both stood there, gazing through the window. Whatever they were saying to each other pleased Daddy. His smile widened and then he leaned over the table to meet her halfway so they could kiss on the lips.

I looked at Clarence.

"Still think that's a business meeting?"

He let his eyes drift down and shook his head.

"Sorry," he said.

"Me too," I replied and turned abruptly.

I walked as quickly as I could. Clarence had to jog to catch up.

"It might still be something innocent," he offered.

"As innocent as Cain's murder of Abel," I replied. The tears in my eyes felt like they were frozen, stuck against my pupils, making the world appear foggy around me.

Mommy's lying sick and broken in a hospital room, was all I could think. It made my throat close.

I crossed the street quickly, nearly running toward the parking lot now.

"It's amazing that you decided to come into the city and be down here just at the right time," Clarence said trying to slow me down.

I stopped abruptly, so abruptly he almost stepped into another pedestrian.

"No, it's not really."

"What do you mean? You knew about this?"

"No. The spirits in the house made me go. The moment I woke up this morning, it was as if someone had whispered in my ear during the night or just before I woke up telling me to go. I felt pushed along."

"You're kidding. Aren't you?"

"No, I'm not. They look after me," I said. I walked on, Clarence hurrying to catch up again.

"You really believe there are spirits in your house? I thought that was just something you wanted people to believe, something we had fun spreading around."

"It is fun, but I do believe it now. Yes," I said. I paused at the entrance to the parking lot. "You'll come over one night this week and go up to the attic with me and decide for yourself."

"Really?"

"Unless you're afraid," I said.

"No," he said shaking his head. He looked back in the direction of the coffee shop and then looked at me again. "No," he repeated, but this time, he didn't sound as confident.

"I've got to stop by the clinic to see my mother," I said. "Will you be all right waiting in the car?"

"Sure."

"Thanks," I said.

One of my frozen tears broke free and trickled icily down my cheek, but I had turned away in time to hide it from Clarence.

I didn't want anyone to see me crying over what Daddy was doing.

Sometimes sadness had to be kept as secret as love.

Sometimes, they were one and the same.

"Don't worry about me," Clarence said after I parked the car at the clinic. "I'll read what I was supposed to read for today's social studies class."

He smiled to give me some warm encouragement. All the way back from the city, I was quiet and didn't respond to any of his attempts to make conversation. I kept seeing Daddy kissing that woman in broad daylight, in a public place, unafraid or unconcerned. Maybe he thought no one knew him there anyway, or maybe he thought what if someone did? What was he or she going to do, call Mommy in the mental clinic to report it?

I nodded at Clarence and stepped out of the car. The partly cloudy day had turned into a nearly overcast sky with a much colder wind blowing into my face. I could feel winter crawling up my spine, its icy fingers sliding over my neck and shoulders. Zipping up my jacket, I started toward the building, not knowing north from south, east from west. I moved like someone in a trance as though the upper part of me was being carried forward against its wishes. Glimpsing myself in the window of another car I passed in the parking lot, I saw how I was holding my shoulders and my head back.

Now, I was sorry I had eaten so much for breakfast. I ate more out of nervousness than hunger, and after seeing Daddy with that woman, all the food in my stomach had turned into balls of lead. It wanted to roll back up my throat and out of my mouth. My legs were so heavy I could barely lift my feet to go up the short stairway to the front doors. I hesitated, took a deep breath, and then entered.

An elderly woman was being escorted through the lobby toward the hallway that led to the elevator. The nurse with her gazed at me and smiled. When the elderly woman saw me, she seized the nurse's hand and stopped walking.

"It's Ida," she cried. She looked like she was an instant away from bursting into happy tears.

"No, no, Rachael. That's not Ida."

"Sure it is. Ida, where have you been? I've been worried sick over you, dear," she told me.

The nurse smiled at me and shook her head.

It was as if there was a button in my head that when pushed would open up the world of pretend. Maybe that was what all actors had in their heads.

"I was away," I said. "I came as soon as I could."

"Oh, dear, dear. I was worried about you, a young woman, all alone in Europe. Did my sister take good care of you?"

"Yes," I said. "And all she did was talk about you."

"Did she? That's nice. You have to tell me all about it," she said.

"She will," the nurse said, "after your nap."

"I will," I promised. "After you rest."

"Good. Don't forget now." She reached for me and I took her withered hand. The fingers were so slim, her paper thin skin seemed to have nothing between it and the bones. Her happiness gave her the strength to squeeze tightly. "I'm so glad you came home, dear. It's just the two of us now, just the two of us."

I smiled at her.

"We'll be fine," I said.

"Yes. We'll be fine." She nodded and then she continued along.

The nurse looked back at me with a smile of gratitude and then led her on toward the elevator.

I had a chill, a shudder running through me for a moment, when I envisioned that old, confused lady could be my mother years from now.

There was a new girl at the reception desk. I didn't pretend to be my mother's sister this time. I told the truth and she called up and then told me to wait because the head nurse was coming down. It put a panic in my chest and for a moment, I couldn't breathe.

"Why? What's wrong?" I demanded.

"Mrs. Fogelman will be here momentarily," the receptionist said. She nodded toward the pair of settees behind me. "Why don't you make yourself comfortable?"

I didn't want to sit, but my legs felt like they might simply melt beneath me, so I moved to the small imitation leather sofa and sat, staring at the elevators. Finally, one opened and a short, stocky woman with dark brown hair looking like it had been trimmed around a bowl, came out and hurriedly walked toward me. I rose.

"You're Mrs. Carlson's daughter?"

"Yes," I said. "What's wrong? Isn't she getting well?"

"I'm Mrs. Fogelman. The doctor was here earlier today and left instructions that I should personally greet any immediate family. There's been a little setback," she said.

"Setback? What does that mean?"

"Isn't your father with you?" she asked instead of answering.

I felt myself tighten like a wire being stretched to its limit. She actually looked past me toward the door.

"Unless he's invisible, I'd have to say no," I told her sharply. "What's wrong with my mother?"

"She's drifted into a comatose state," Mrs. Fogelman revealed after a moment of indecision. "However, the doctor feels it is only a temporary condition. We've moved her to our intensive care area and we're monitoring her carefully. I thought the doctor had reached your father and that's why you were here," she added.

"No, I think my father is unreachable at the moment," I muttered. "Can I see her, please?"

She nodded.

"Yes, that might be very good. She should hear your voice," Mrs. Fogelman decided. She smiled and we walked to the elevator.

"Are you in high school or college?" she asked me when the doors closed.

I hadn't been in many elevators in my life, but I always hated the deep silence, the way everyone avoided looking directly at anyone else, and waited uncomfortably for the doors to open again. The quiet moments seemed to put everyone on edge as if being closed in a small area with other human beings was alien to our species.

I barely heard Mrs. Fogelman talking.

"High school," I muttered. Who cares? I thought. What difference did that make now? What difference did anything make now?

She smiled at me and the doors opened mercifully one floor up. She led me down the corridor to the ICU ward and then to my mother's bedside. Her eyes were shut tight, the corners wrinkled.

"She looks like she's in great pain," I moaned.

Mrs. Fogelman didn't deny it.

"Mental pain," she said, trying to make it sound like it wasn't as bad as physical pain, but there was no hiding the truth. Mommy was in agony.

I reached for her hand and held it tightly in mine. Then I leaned over the bed railing and wiped some strands of hair from her forehead.

"Mommy, it's me, Cinnamon. Please, wake up, Mommy. Please."

Her face seemed frozen in that grimace of anguish. Her lips were stretched and white.

"What are you doing for her?" I demanded.

"We've got to be patient," Mrs. Fogelman said. "She'll snap out of it soon."

"What if she doesn't?"

"She will," she insisted, but my urgency and concern made her sound less confident.

"Do they always snap out of it?" When she didn't respond, I said, "Well?"

"Let's not think the worst, dear. The doctor is watching her closely. Keep talking to her," she advised and walked away quickly to get herself behind the sanctity of the central desk where she busied herself with other things and glanced my way only occasionally.

"Mommy," I pleaded, "please get better. You've got to get better and come home. I need you. We've got to be together again.

"Grandmother is taking over the house, just as you always feared. I want you to come home and make her put everything back the way it was. Please, Mommy. Please get better."

I sat there pleading with her until I felt my throat dry up and close. Then I kissed her on the cheek and looked at her face. Her eyelids fluttered and stopped.

"How are you doing, dear?" Mrs. Fogelman asked, coming up behind me.

I shook my head.

"Is your father on his way?" she asked.

I stared at her, bit down on my lip, and then smiled.

"The moment he gets an opportunity," I told her. "He'll rush right over."

She stared at me. Hadn't I said it right?

Or was it the rapid and constant flow of tears over my cheeks and chin that confused her?

I flicked them off, smiled at her again, looked back at Mommy and fled.

Clarence was so involved in his reading he didn't hear or see me until I opened the car door. By then, I had stopped crying, but he couldn't miss my red eyes.

"What's wrong?" he asked.

"She's worse. She's in a coma."

"Oh no. What do they say?"

I looked at him.

"They say what they're supposed to say. They say, 'Don't worry.' They say pretend this isn't happening. They say go on with your life and ignore it, ignore all of it, put on a good act, recite your lines, stay in the spotlights so you can't see the audience."

I started the car.

I saw rather than heard him mouth a curse.

I drove him home. He kept asking me what I was going to do now and I kept saying, "I don't know." He especially wanted to know if I was going to confront my father with what we had seen today.

"Would you?" I asked him.

He thought a moment and shrugged.

"I probably wouldn't be as surprised by it as you are," he finally replied. "But I'd like to help you," he said when I pulled up to his house. "Just don't be afraid to ask me for anything."

"Thanks, Clarence."

"Am I still coming over tomorrow night to meet your spirits?"

I smiled at him.

"Sure," I said. "We'll talk about it in school."

"I'll call you later," he promised. He leaned over to kiss my left cheek and then got out. I watched him walk away. He paused at his front door to wave goodbye and then I drove home. I don't know how I managed it. The car must have known the way by itself. One moment I blinked and the next I was pulling up the driveway.

The house never looked as lonely and dark to me as it did now. I didn't go inside. Instead, I walked around to the rear and then up to the knoll where the Demerests were buried. I stood before the old tombstones remembering the times Mommy and I were here.

The wind was blowing harder, the sky looking more bruised and angry, reflecting my mood. I could feel the cold rain threatening. We might even have flurries tonight, I thought, but I ignored the frigid air. Anger made my blood hot anyway. I could never understand the rage Medea felt toward her husband, Jason, when he betrayed her in the Greek tragedy. Now, I thought I could.

I charged toward a broken tree branch, scooped it up and dug into the ground, scratching away the earth like some madwoman searching for buried treasure. Finally, exhausted, I stopped. The hole was big enough for what I wanted anyway.

I reached around my neck and undid the charm necklace Daddy had bought me on my sixteenth birthday. I dropped it into the hole and covered it up.

It was as if I was burying him.

I jammed the stick into the ground like a grave marker and then I walked away without a backward glance.

5

Surprised by Love

The stillness in the house greeted me like a slap in the face. Grandmother Beverly's car was here, which meant she was home, but I didn't hear the television droning or any sounds coming from the kitchen. Was she already asleep? Good, I thought. I didn't want to face her at the moment. I started up the stairs, my head down, and lifted it only when I turned the knob on my bedroom door and was shocked to discover it wouldn't open.

It wouldn't open because a lock and a hasp had been installed and the lock was closed.

Both amazed and confused, I stepped back and cried, "What?" I had to touch it to believe it was really there. A lock on my own door?

"Grandmother!" I screamed. I spun around, but she didn't appear. I marched to her bedroom door and threw it open. She wasn't in her room, so I charged back to the stairway and pounded my way down, spinning at the bottom and rushing to the living room door.

There she was, seated comfortably like some queen mother, waiting for me.

"Why is there a lock on my door?"

She glared at me, her eyes small but so full of anger they looked capable of shooting out small flames in my direction.

"Where have you been today — and don't make up any ridiculous story about going to the hospital to be with your mother," she quickly warned. "I'm talking about the whole day from the moment you rushed out of this house without breakfast until now. Well?" she demanded, holding her body stiffly forward.

"Why are you asking me that and how dare you put a lock on my bedroom door?" I flared back at her, flashing my eyes with temper as hot and red as hers.

She sat back, a cold twisted smirk on her face.

"First, I'm asking because the school called here looking for you. Apparently, someone there was concerned about you and wanted to know how you were and why you weren't at school," she revealed.

Miss Hamilton, I thought to myself.

"Can you even begin to imagine how embarrassed I was when I had to reveal you weren't home and I didn't have any idea where you were?

"I called your father," she added, nodding. "I had to, of course."

"Really?" I replied, folding my arms under my breasts and placing my weight on my right foot, "and what did he have to say?"

"Fortunately for you, I was unable to reach him at the time."

"Is that so? Why? What did they tell you? Was he with a client, at a meeting, what?"

"That has nothing to do with our situation," she said. "Where were you?"

"Why is there a lock on my door?" I asked instead of answering.

"I put that lock on your door so you couldn't do what you always do when I question you or try to guide you . . . run off to your room and lock yourself inside. I'll unlock it when you tell me the truth. Now, where were you?"

"How dare you do this, Grandmother? That's my room!" I shouted at her, tears burning my eyelids.

"Until your mother returns, I have to be the one in charge of you, responsible for you. You are still a minor and your father is a very busy man with a great deal on his mind these days."

"Oh, yes," I said shaking my head, "my father is a very, very busy man. He's too busy to visit my mother. He's too busy to know she's fallen into a coma. That's a very busy man," I said.

"Mothers and daughters have to realize that their husbands and fathers can't be at their beck and call every minute. They're out there in the hard, cold world trying to make a living, trying to earn enough to provide and keep you comfortable. Who do you think pays the mortgage on this ridiculous relic of a house, and who pays for the food you eat and the gas you waste driving around in that car of yours, and who gave you that car and who —"

"And who cares?" I shouted, covering my ears with my hands. "Take it all back, everything!"

I turned and fled from her. When I reached my bedroom door again, I tried to pull the lock off, but I couldn't do it. Who could have ever imagined her doing something like this? Did meanness make people more inventive?

Instead of continuing my confrontation with her, I went up to the attic and threw myself on the small settee where I curled up in a fetal position and closed my eyes. My pounding heart calmed. The emotional tension had drained my body of all of its energy. I pulled the old afghan over myself, closed my eyes and almost immediately fell asleep.

The sound of my name hours and hours later woke me, but not abruptly. For a few moments it was as if the sound was inside me, in some dream, echoing. I groaned, my eyelids fluttered and then I felt someone touch my shoulder and I opened my eyes to see Daddy.

"Cinnamon. What are you doing?" he asked. "What in the world is going on here?"

I stared at him. Was this a dream? He had been in this attic so rarely that the sight of him here was more like a phantom of my imagination.

When I was a little girl, I could look at him and think my daddy was the perfect daddy, so handsome and warm, so loving and full of magic. There was magic in those hazel eyes.

They could twinkle and make sickness go away, aches and pains flee, colds disappear and most of all, sad moments pop like bubbles. I remember his laughter. It was more like a song and whenever he said my name, it sounded like poetry. But that all seemed so long ago, truly like a dream, a fantasy. The memories were challenged now, cross-examined and scrutinized through my older, far more critical and discerning eyes.

His smiles were not as warm and held as long as I had thought. His words were not as soft and as comforting as I had wished. His promises were often forgotten, words written in the snow, melted and erased by the first touch of probing sunlight. He was merely a man.

I sat up, grinding my eyes to pull back the veil of sleepiness.

"Grandmother put a lock on my bedroom door," I said.

He stood up.

"I know. She told me about your not attending school today. Where were you? What did you do?"

"She put a lock on my bedroom door," I repeated, annoyed by the quivering in my voice.

"It's off," he said. "I unlocked it and took it off. Now, tell me where you were. What's going on with you?"

I looked up at him. The words were there, waiting to be born, launched at him like tiny knives. But I couldn't do it. I couldn't do it because saying them, sending them at him would cut me to pieces as well. I could only tremble at the thought of what it would all be like afterward with all of the ugly truth spilled before us.

"Don't you feel well?" he asked.

"No," I said.

"Well, why didn't you just tell Grandmother that?"

"She put a lock on my door," I muttered.

"I told you. I took it off," he said. "Where did you go?"

"Mommy's in a coma. Do you know that?" I snapped back at him.

He closed his eyes and nodded.

"I know. That's where I've been since I left work. The doctor assures me she will recuperate. He thinks it's just a temporary thing. She could be very much better tomorrow."

"Could she?"

"Yes. Now what did you do today, Cinnamon?"

"I had to be by myself today," I lied.

"We're all going through a very difficult time, Cinnamon. We've got to be strong, strong for Mommy," he said.

I couldn't look at him. I kept my eyes fixed on the floor. I thought I could hear my spirits, the Demerest women, all laughing at him. I guess it made me smile.

"Why are you laughing at what I'm saying?" he demanded. "Cinnamon, if you persist in this behavior, I'll have to have you examined by a doctor, too," he threatened.

That really made me laugh and made him furious.

"Go to your room," he ordered, "and you had better be in school tomorrow and behave or I'll take the car away from you. I mean it."

"Who pays for the mortgage and for the food and for the gas I waste . . ."

"What? You're not making any sense, Cinnamon. Go to bed," he ordered and turned away quickly.

I think he was actually afraid of me.

I sat there for a while, listening to the soft murmuring of the voices in the walls, the comforting rhythm of their words. A hundred years ago they came up here to escape from sadness too, I thought.

How little really has changed.

Daddy did take the lock off, but the hasp remained as a reminder of my grandmother's fury and power. She muttered around me all throughout breakfast the next day and followed me out of the house with a trail of warnings and threats, trying to make me feel guilty for putting more pressure and turmoil on our family at a difficult time.

"You're not the only one who's suffering here, Cinnamon. Think of your father having all this on his head and having to have to do a good job at work at the same time. I know it's difficult for young people to be considerate of others these days. They've been spoiled and turned into self-centered little creatures, but I expect more from you."

Before I left, I couldn't resist turning on her and saying, "I'm not the self-centered one here, Grandmother. You should direct yourself more at Daddy," I fired. She raised her eyebrows and chased after me, out of the house and to the car.

"And what is that supposed to mean, young lady? What are you saying now? How can you say such a thing? Well?"

"Ask him," I said and got into my car.

I left her standing there, fuming.

Clarence was waiting for me at the lockers in the hallway when I arrived at school. One glance at his face told me something was very wrong.

"What?" I asked instead of saying hello or good morning.

"They called my mother at work," he said. "Told her I wasn't at school. She called my father and I'm grounded for a month. I can't go anywhere on the weekends."

"Oh. Sorry," I said. "They called my house too. Who knew they cared?" I added and pulled what I needed from my locker.

Clarence smiled.

"Get ready for the wisecracks," he said. "My sister already warned me they're talking about us."

"Good." I put my arm through his. "Let's

give them something to really talk about then."

He looked surprised, but happy.

There wasn't an eye not directed at us as we made our way to homeroom. And that was the way it remained most of the day. We could see them all whispering, giggling, rotating their eyes with their fantasies and stories about us. I could tell Clarence was becoming more embarrassed by it than I was, but whenever he was embarrassed, his earlobes would turn red. The rest of him would grow pale and he would keep his eyes down, his lower lip under his upper.

None of the girls in my classes had the nerve to confront me directly. Even the girls who were so much bigger physically shied away from any face-to-face confrontation. Everyone was afraid of the evil eye, as my penetrating dark glare was called. The boys, however, were different. Eddie Morris, who liked to tease Clarence anyway, was full of witty remarks like, "Viagra Boy, can you keep up with her?"

Before lunch, Eddie and his buddies surrounded Clarence and tormented him with questions about our relationship. I was a little late because Miss Hamilton approached me in the hallway and practically shoved the script of her new school play into my hands.

"I want you to try out for the lead," she insisted. "Don't say no or anything until you read the play and see the part, Cinnamon. Please," she cajoled and I nodded and took it.

When I reached the cafeteria, Clarence was

trying to get by four boys led by Eddie. Eddie kept poking him in the shoulder, baiting him with questions like, "Does she paint her nipples black too?"

Clarence lifted his eyes to see me coming and then, without any warning, swung his closed fist around and caught Eddie Morris on the side of his head. It took him by such surprise, he lost his balance and fell, spilling his books and notebooks over the floor. His friends, shocked, stepped back and Mr. Jacobs, the teacher on lunch duty, came charging forward, inserting himself quickly between Clarence and Eddie who was rising in a fury to retaliate.

He marched them both past me toward the principal's office. When Clarence went by, I caught a gleeful smile in his eyes.

"The spirits made me do it," he muttered and I laughed.

The other boys took one look at me and cleared away quickly. When Clarence returned, he came directly to my table and told me he had gotten a severe warning and two days detention.

"They're sending a letter home to good old Mom and Dad," he added, "but they don't have to. My sister will be blabbing about it at the dinner table tonight. Maybe my father will be at one of his famous dinner meetings. Maybe they both will be."

As it turned out, that was exactly what happened. Clarence called me to tell me so. Then he surprised me by asking when he should come over.

"I thought you were grounded," I said.

"I'll tell them I had to study with you for a math test or something. That usually works. Any excuse usually works," he added. "Ours is a house built on a foundation of lies everyone accepts."

"Come any time," I said and went to join my grandmother for dinner. It was the first time since Mommy had been taken away by ambulance.

But I was feeling better about Mommy because when I called the hospital, the nurse in ICU told me she had snapped out of the coma and was being moved back to a regular room. She said the doctor wanted to hold off visitors until the next day so she could get a full night's rest, but he was speaking with much more positive notes. It filled my heart with enough hope and warmth to even face my grandmother and be civil. The end, after all, was in sight. The madness in the house would stop.

What happened with Daddy was something else, something to postpone, but in my secret heart of hearts, I prayed there was some explanation and some end to that betrayal as well. Funny, I thought, how good news could turn you into a child again, permitting you to believe in happy endings.

At eight o'clock, the doorbell rang and I hurried down the stairs to get there before Grand-mother Beverly. Daddy, who had called earlier to tell her he was attending an important business meeting, was not home for dinner and wouldn't be until quite late.

"Hi," I said after I opened the door and found Clarence standing there, looking shy and afraid. Was I the first girl he had ever visited?

He turned to gaze down the driveway as if he thought he might have been followed and then nodded, smiled and stepped into the house. His eyes were like hungry little creatures gobbling up everything in sight.

"Those two bare areas were where my mother had her favorite paintings," I said nodding toward the wall where Mommy's New Orleans paintings once hung. "Grandmother Beverly is in the process of replacing them with something more cheerful," I said under my breath. "When Mommy comes home, we'll put her pictures back."

He nodded and then stiffened and froze as Grandmother Beverly came out of the kitchen to see who had come to the door. The instant her gaze fell on him, her face expressed her disapproval: her lips stretching and flowing into the corners, her eyes flashing disgust. Clarence was wearing a ragged looking old bomber jacket and a tee-shirt with a picture of Bach and the words *Fugue Me* written beneath it.

"And who is this?"

"This is Clarence Baron, Grandmother. He

and I are studying for a social studies test we're taking tomorrow. Is that all right with you?"

"Why didn't you ask before he arrived?" she countered.

"I couldn't imagine any reason why you wouldn't approve," I replied as sweetly as I could manage. "Maybe you've heard of Clarence's father, Michael Baron, one of the most prominent attorneys in the area."

She drew her head back as if she had flies in her nose and scrutinized Clarence as if she were considering him for a part in her play.

"Don't stay too late," she commanded, gave Clarence a threatening look of warning, and then returned to the kitchen.

I smiled at him.

"Now you see why she was the inspiration for the character of Freddy in *A Nightmare on Elm Street*," I said.

Clarence laughed and I hooked my arm into his and steered him toward the staircase.

"Quick, before she decides to take a sample of your blood," I said and hurriedly moved us up. I was embarrassed about the hasp on my bedroom door so I rushed him by and took him directly to the attic. I lit a stick of incense while he waited in the doorway, gazing in nervously.

"Don't worry. There's nothing here that will hurt you," I promised.

"I know that," he said, but not with great confidence, and entered.

"This was a favorite place for my mother and

113

me," I began and then showed him the old pictures my mother had found, rattling off the names we knew and the names we had created, as well as a line or two about them, which was also mostly imagined.

"She is my favorite," I said showing him the picture of Jonathan Demerest's youngest daughter Belva. Clarence held it and studied her faint visage. Even awash in the sepia tint, her big eyes stood out.

"She looks so sad for a young girl," he said.

"Well, she fell in love with a young officer in her father's regiment, Captain Lance Arnold, and he fell in love with her even though she was only thirteen at the time."

"Thirteen? Really?"

"Yes. In those days women were engaged or married before they were twenty, you know."

"How old was he?"

"Twenty-three. Captain Arnold courted her and finally won her father's blessing. They were married when she was only fifteen and less then a year later, she was pregnant, but she and her baby died in a horrible birthing. Captain Arnold killed himself in grief."

"You're kidding?" Clarence said.

I wiped a tear from my cheek and shook my head. Then I took the picture from him and stared at it.

"She wrote exquisite but sad poems mourning the short life of beautiful things. She was a very sensitive person who liked to wander through the fields and forest and talk to the animals."

I closed my eyes and recited, "The color of roses lives in my eyes long after they have faded and gone. I lock the scent within my heart and when I sleep, they bloom once more."

I sighed and then looked at Clarence. He seemed about to cry himself. His eyes shone brilliantly with unused tears.

"Wow," he said.

"Sometimes, I really feel her beside me," I whispered. "When I'm very sad and alone, I close my eyes and I sense her fingers moving against mine."

I put my hand on Clarence's and he jerked back.

"You're kidding?"

"No," I said. "It's true. You can feel the love and the energy they left here. Close your eyes," I told him. "Relax and put everything out of your mind. Just conjure up her face. Go on," I urged and took his hand again. He let me hold his fingers and draw him closer to me.

We sat together, our eyes closed, holding hands, listening to our own hearts beat.

"Belva," I whispered. Then I leaned over and kissed him on the cheek.

He acted as if he had been stung.

"Why did you do that?"

"I couldn't help it. Belva made me do it," I said. "She takes me over sometimes. I think she sees you as her young captain when he was first courting her. She gets excited again and full of joy. Do you feel anything inside you?"

He cocked his head, considering.

"What should I feel?" he asked.

"A strange warmth, but a pleasant warmth. When you look at me, what do you see?" I asked bringing my face closer. "Look into my eyes, deeply."

He nodded.

"Yeah, I see what you mean, I think."

"Yes, you do," I told him. "I feel it, too. They're in us, taking us over."

I kissed him on the lips and then I did it again and he moved closer and put his arm around me, drawing me into him. I started to lie back, unbuttoning my blouse as I did so. He hovered over me, his eyes full of excitement, amazed. I reached up for him, drawing his face toward me, his lips to my breasts. He kissed me and for a moment I held onto him as if I were drowning. He moved completely over me and we kissed again and again.

"Wait," I said and sat up to strip off my blouse. I wasn't wearing a bra.

"God, you're beautiful, Cinnamon. I've been afraid to say it, but I always thought so. Right from the first time I set eyes on you."

"Yes. Captain Arnold said something just like that to Belva," I told him. "Don't you see? It's happening just the way it happened to them. We must make love," I decided. "We must make this night the most special night of our lives and then hold it in our hearts forever and ever."

He nodded and started to undress. I slipped my jeans down and moments later, both of us naked, we embraced. We kissed until we were breathless and then, as if coming to his senses, Clarence pulled away abruptly.

"I could get you in trouble," he said. He shook his head. "I feel like Mrs. Miller is standing next to us, warning us about safe sex like she does in health education. I'm not exactly prepared for this."

I smiled at him.

"You're always the gentleman, sir, considerate as well as loving. That's what Belva said to her captain."

"I want to make love to you, Cinnamon, more than anything," he said mournfully.

"Me too, but you're right, Captain."

He laughed.

"Wait," I said. "I have an idea."

I rose, wrapped the afghan around me and told him I'd be right back. He covered himself with his jacket. I tiptoed out of the attic, down the short stairway to Mommy and Daddy's room. Long ago, I had gone in there curious and explored. I discovered where Daddy kept his contraceptives. They were still where I had first found them. As soon as I had one, I rushed back to the attic.

Clarence was exactly where and how I had left him as if he feared a movement no matter how slight in either direction would shatter the magic. I stepped before him and opened my hand. His eyes widened. He reached for the contraceptive and turned to put it on while I slipped back beside him on the settee. Then he moved over me, lingering for a moment.

"I've fantasized about this so much, it feels unreal."

"It's real," I whispered. I put my hands around the back of his neck and drew his lips down to mine. It was a long, passionate, wonderful kiss.

"Oh Captain, my special, private, wonderful Captain," I whispered. "Take me to paradise."

There were moments when I thought maybe Clarence was right: I was making love in a dream. It did seem unreal, ethereal, but my blood was stirred by my pounding, hungry heart, a heart starving for love, for real affection, for warmth. My head echoed with our moans of pleasure, our reaching out for each other, into each other. I was afraid it would stop and when it did, I came down from my ecstasy reluctantly.

He softened and relaxed over me, his breath slowing until he was able to raise himself away and look into my face.

"Cinnamon," he said.

"No," I said putting my finger on his lips. "Call me Belva. I am Belva."

He smiled.

"Belva. I — I really love you."

"I'm glad, Captain. Now take me away from

here," I said. "Take me someplace wonderful where we will always be happy."

"Okay," he said smiling.

I moved over a little and he scrunched down beside me. I pulled the afghan over us and told him to rest and be still and enjoy our wonderful, blissful aftermath. He closed his eyes. We held each other and soon, we fell asleep.

Grandmother Beverly's screams shattered our dreams. She was in the attic doorway, grimacing with revulsion, her eyes big, her mouth twisted.

"What depraved and despicable thing are you doing?" she cried.

Clarence trembled as if the house itself was shaking.

"Get out!" I screamed back at her. "This is my private place. Get out!"

"I knew it! I knew when I didn't hear a sound that you were wallowing in sin. Disgusting — and in your own home, right above my head."

I leaped up from the settee, forgetting my nudity, and closed the attic door in her face.

Clarence was rushing to get dressed.

"Oh wow, sorry," he said. "I'd better go. I fell asleep. I'm sorry."

"There's nothing to be sorry about. She had no right to spy on us."

I started to dress.

"You going to be all right?" he asked when he got his shoes on and reached for his jacket.

"I'll be peachy keen as always. Don't worry

about it, Clarence. This is a glass house. The people in it can't throw stones."

He nodded and reached for the doorknob. I guess I couldn't blame him for being terrified. I hurriedly completed my own dressing and walked him down to the front entrance. Then I stepped outside. It had started to rain so we remained under the portico.

"I'll meet you at the lockers in the morning."

"Yes."

He kissed me quickly.

"Night," he said.

"Good night, Clarence. Clarence," I called when he stepped down. He turned.

"Yes?"

"You made a wonderful Captain Arnold."

He smiled and shrugged.

"Maybe I should go out for the play, too."

"Maybe," I said and watched him get into his car and drive away.

Then I turned and reentered the house. Grandmother Beverly was standing in the shadows. She stepped into the light so that the glow of the chandelier washed the darkness off her face. It glowed like ivory, her eyes twirling with anger.

"Your father will hear of this," she promised.

"Yes," I said, "and when you tell him, ask him what's worse, what I did or what he did? Ask him if adultery is worse," I threw back at her.

She raised her hands to the base of her throat.

"That's . . . a lie, but even so," she added quickly, "you're still a minor and . . ."

"I'm not a child, Grandmother. A hundred years ago, women were married and had children by my age. I'm a woman and what makes me age is not time. What makes me age is what the so-called adults around me do, to me, in spite of me. They won't let us be children. They kill the child in us quickly and then they ask us to be grown-ups like they are.

"I'd rather live in my attic," I spat and left her still mostly in the shadows, glaring out at me like some owl in the darkness waiting for easier prey.

I sprawled on my bed and gazed up at the ceiling until I felt my heart slow and my body calm down. Then I reached for the script Miss Hamilton had given me. It was a play entitled *Death Takes a Holiday*. I was familiar with the story. It was one of Mommy's favorites, actually.

A young woman is courted by a handsome man who turns out to be Death on holiday and when it's time for him to leave, he tells her who he is and she reveals she always knew and she's still willing to go with him.

Romantic slop?

Maybe.

But at the moment, I would gladly put my hand into his and run off.

I could do this part well, I thought.

I could do it so well, I'd frighten myself.

6

Seizing the Stage

Grandmother Beverly didn't tell Daddy about Clarence and me. She had a better way and a far more effective place to snap her punitive whip. Now it was Clarence's turn to be called out of class, only for him it was to meet with his father. Because Clarence didn't return for his afternoon classes, I didn't find out about it until I returned from visiting with Mommy. Instinctively, I knew something terrible was going on. Every time I thought about him, about our teacher calling out his name and telling him to report to the office, I felt my heart thump along like a flat tire.

When I drove into the clinic parking lot and entered the building, I tried to push my anxieties under a blanket of smiles. The last thing I wanted to do was lay my problems at Mommy's hospital bed. For her sake, everything had to look pleasant. She was a weakened vessel sailing in a tumultuous sea. Adding the weight of my problems to her own might sink her for good.

She had just finished having a cup of tea and was still sitting up in her bed. I could see from the brightness in her eyes that she had crossed through the darkness between her heart-breaking memories and the present. She still looked quite fragile, her lips trembling slightly, like the lips of someone on the verge of opening a dam of tears, but there was a significant change in her demeanor. It brightened my own spirits and I rushed to her side.

"Mommy, you're better," I cried and threw my arms around her. I kissed her and she did start to shed some tears.

"I was asking for you, Cinnamon," she said. "They told me some silly story about my younger sister coming here."

I laughed, and held her hand.

"That was me, Mommy. I pretended to be your sister the first time I visited."

She shook her head.

"Why?"

"I don't know," I said shifting my eyes guiltily.

She stared at me, her own eyes filling with understanding.

"Who wants to have a mother in here?" she asked gazing around. "I know how you feel." She sighed, closed her eyes and lowered herself to her pillow. "I lost the baby, Cinnamon. I lost her."

"It wasn't your fault, Mommy. You did every-thing the doctor told you to do."

She nodded.

"It wasn't meant to be," she said in a

whisper. "Grandmother Beverly was right."

"No, she wasn't right. She's never right."

Mommy shook her head.

"This time, I'm afraid she was. Maybe I was too old. I had this hope that having a baby would make us a better family, improve my relationship with your father. Sometimes, you just can't force fate. It's almost a sin to try."

"Stop it, Mommy. Don't do this to yourself. That's why you were . . . sick before."

"Sick?" She nodded. "Yes, I suppose you could call it that. I don't remember very much. I found myself here and all they tell me is I suffered a slight nervous breakdown, but that I'm on the way to a full recovery. What happened, Cinnamon? What did I do that they would put me in here?"

I shook my head. Was I supposed to tell her?

"Please, honey. We don't keep things from each other," she reminded me.

"You thought you hadn't had the baby. You thought you were having labor pains."

I decided to leave out the bizarre drawing she had made on her body.

"Oh."

"Then you thought you gave birth prematurely and the baby was in intensive care. You kept asking me how she was."

She nodded, took a deep breath to keep her tears back, and shook her head.

"Is your father terribly upset?" she asked.

If I have any acting skills, I thought, now

we'll see. My slight hesitation already had triggered some concern in her and her eyes snapped open and turned to peruse my face.

"He's been working harder to keep himself from thinking about it all," I said. "I haven't seen much of him."

She nodded.

"I don't blame him for working harder and not wanting to think about it. He wanted the baby very much."

I nodded, smiled and took her hand again.

"You must get stronger and come home as quickly as you can, Mommy. I need you."

Her eyebrows rose at the urgency in my voice.

"Grandmother Beverly making things hard for you?"

"Let's just say you've got a lot to do at home, Mommy," I replied and she laughed.

"Let her have her moment in the sun, gloat about what happened and how right she was. That's all she has, all she's ever had: her own self-righteousness," Mommy added. I felt my heart fill with joy. We were conspirators again, a team, turning the world into our stage, putting the lights where we wanted them, designing the set, filling it with our own props, writing the script as we went along.

"You mean you won't ignore her as much?"

"Exactly. I'll do exactly the opposite: pay too much attention to her. We'll agree with her, but of course, we won't."

"We'll haunt her. We'll even ask her opinions," I suggested.

She smiled gleefully.

"About every little thing, anything."

"Weigh her down with more responsibilities, more decisions."

"We'll yes her to death," Mommy said. "We'll overwhelm her with respect and cooperation until she runs off exhausted into the wings."

I laughed.

"Oh Mommy, I can't wait for you to come home."

She asked me about school and I told her about the play and Miss Hamilton's giving me a script.

"It's a wonderful play. Do go out for it, honey. I'd love to see you on the stage, a real stage with a real audience and not just our little attic room of make-believe, okay?"

"I'll think about it," I said.

"Good." She closed her eyes. "Good."

Her condition made it possible for her to turn on sleep in an instant. I saw her breathing become regular, slow, and felt her grip on my hand soften. Gently, I pulled away and sat back, watching her for a while.

She's coming home, I thought. Mommy's coming home.

I left the hospital with bounce in my steps. I felt I could do battle with anyone or anything again. I would go out for the play. I wouldn't be afraid of competing. I could even handle Grandmother Beverly until Mommy came home, and as for Daddy . . . I would pretend I knew nothing and let his own conscience boil in his heart.

Grandmother Beverly was in the kitchen, preparing dinner. I hated to admit it, but the aroma of the roast chicken and baked potatoes made me hungry. It all smelled so good. She greeted me and told me Daddy was coming home and would visit Mommy after dinner.

"So we're eating as soon as he arrives," she informed me. "Put your things away and come down to set the table."

"Mommy's better," I told her. "She's a lot better."

She nodded.

"I know all about it," she said as if that was the least important thing and went back to preparing dinner.

I hurried upstairs. I wouldn't return to the hospital with Daddy later, I thought. I didn't want to ride with him. I was afraid I wouldn't be able to keep what I knew to myself. Anyway, tomorrow were the auditions for the play and I did want to study the part, even memorize some of it to impress everyone.

Just as I put my books down and started to change my clothes, the phone rang. It was Clarence.

"I'm sorry I didn't call you sooner," I told him as soon as I heard his voice. "I went right to the hospital. My mother is better. She'll be coming home soon. She's better, Clarence."

"I'm glad," he said, but the heavy tone in his voice told me something was very, very wrong.

"What happened? Why did your father come to school for you?"

"Your grandmother called him this morning at the office," he said.

My heart stopped and started.

"What?"

"She told him everything she saw. She threatened all sorts of things, including a lawsuit. All this after I cut school and he had grounded me, too," he added. "Then he saw the letter about my fighting and it was like lighting a wick on a stick of dynamite. I never saw him this angry. My mother's just as angry. They had a meeting about me and they've decided to send me to the Brooks Academy. My father's always threatened to do that."

"Boarding school? When?"

"Immediately," he said.

"How can they do that?"

"You don't know my father. When he makes up his mind, he goes to work and moves mountains out of his way." Clarence took a breath. "I'm leaving tomorrow."

"Tomorrow! You're kidding?"

"I wish I was," he said.

"Well, why are you going? Don't go, Clarence."

"I've got to go. They've already removed

me from school here."

"But —"

"He even suggested he might send me to a military school if I don't cooperate."

"Oh, Clarence."

"Maybe you can come up to Brooks once in a while. It's only about two and a half-hours' drive. I'll call you whenever I can, too. I can take my computer. Maybe we can e-mail each other every day."

"My grandmother did this," I groaned.

"I never saw my father as angry or afraid of anything or anyone."

I was quiet. I didn't know what to say. Who could I turn to for help and sympathy? My father? Hardly. I couldn't tell Mommy about this yet. I had to give her a chance to fully recover. Never did I feel as trapped and alone. I held the receiver to my ear, but Clarence was becoming fainter and fainter, a voice drifting away, a face diminishing, a memory thinning until it was nearly impossible to revive. He was on a boat floating into the darkness.

"I'm sorry," was all I could offer.

"I'll call as soon as I can," was his weak and despondent reply.

When I hung up, I felt as if I had closed my last window and was shut up in a room with no door.

"Cinnamon!" I heard Grandmother shout up the stairs. "Set the table. It's getting late."

You have no idea how late it is, Grand-mother, I thought. No idea.

I decided to say nothing about Clarence at dinner. I wouldn't give her the satisfaction of knowing she had succeeded in getting exactly what she intended. Daddy was buoyant when he returned. He knew about Mommy's re-covery, of course, and talked about how we were going to make things pleasant for her when she came home.

"When she's stronger, we can think about a nice little holiday, perhaps. In the spring. She's always wanted to go to Disney World. What do you think?"

"Ridiculous," Grandmother Beverly said. "Adults wanting to go to a children's playland."

"It's not only for children. Besides, the child in you never should die," Daddy countered.

I raised my eyebrows. It was rare to see or hear him disagree with her.

"You'll like it too, Mom," he said.

"Me? You want me to go to Disney World?"

"Why not? You'd be surprised at how you would enjoy it."

"Surprised for sure," she said.

He turned to me, smiling. "I spoke with Mommy late today and she told me you said you were going out for the school play."

"Maybe," I said.

"It would make her happy," he told me.

I glared at him.

"I know what makes her happy and what doesn't, Daddy. I know better than anyone."

His smile held, but lost its glow.

"Sure you do, Cinnamon. I know that." He glanced at Grandmother Beverly.

"What do you think, Mom?"

"She dresses like she's on some stage anyway," she said. "And she certainly needs more to do. Idle time leads to trouble," she added turning to me, her eyes small and hot with accusation.

I looked away, my lips struggling to open, my tongue thrashing about, anxious to fire off the furious words.

Don't give her the satisfaction, I told myself. Pretend nothing she does or says can have an effect on you. Defeat her with indifference.

That took all the control I could muster. Perhaps it was my greatest performance.

I smiled at both of them.

"Yes, I have decided," I said. "I'm going to win that part and be in the play."

"Good," Daddy said clapping his hands. "I have something wonderful to tell your mother tonight."

Of course, it was easier for me to say it, but even with Miss Hamilton's encouragement, winning the part was going to be a formidable task. The two other girls who I knew were going out for it were both veterans of the school's stage. One of them was Iris Ainsley, the prettiest girl in the senior class by far. I had to admit to myself that she looked the part more than I did. She had soft hair the color of fresh corn and eyes that looked as though God had taken them from the purest sapphire. She was an inch or so shorter than I was, but she had a dream figure, lithe with soft turns from her neck to her shoulders. When she walked through the school, she seemed to float. It was easy to see the looks of appreciation and longing in the eyes of some of the male teachers as well as the boys in school. She had a very pleasant speaking voice and she was an honor student.

If I had anything over her, it was my stronger desire to win the part, to win it for Mommy. Iris didn't have the same hunger, the same need and determination. She couldn't raise herself to the level of intensity. She was too comfortable being Iris Ainsley to really step out of herself and be the woman in the play. I only hoped others saw it as I did.

Auditions were held after school in the auditorium. I had been having a horrendous day. Rumors encircled me like a ring of fire now that everyone knew Clarence had been taken out of school. A little truth was mixed with a lot of exaggeration to create a recipe for disgrace. My role attracted the most exaggeration, especially from the lips of the boys. According to what some of the kids were saying, I had either raped poor innocent Clarence or taught him some nasty satanic rituals. Dirty remarks were cast my way in the halls and in the cafeteria. I found disgusting notes on my desk and shoved into my locker. I ignored it all and kept my focus on what I had to do: remain within that spotlight so that I couldn't see the world around me.

Most of the students who were going out for the play looked genuinely surprised I was there. Miss Hamilton handed out scenes from the play. She began by explaining the story and setting up the characters.

"Don't think about one character or another. Just read what I give you to read and leave it up to me to decide who fits each character the best. I appreciate you all coming out; it takes courage. And I would like to state right now that if you don't find yourself with a part, please consider being a member of our set crew, prop crew, lighting crew or publicity committee. My advice to all of you is to get involved any way you can," she added looking directly at me.

It filled me with dread. Was it a foregone conclusion that Iris would get the part I longed to have?

The readings began. Iris had done what I had done: she had memorized the lead's lines. I could see from their faces that everyone assumed she was going to get the role. I felt it was almost futile when I was called. The others didn't smile with disdain as much as they

133

stared with curiosity. None of them had ever seen me do anything in front of an audience. I read in class, of course, and I made reports when I had to, just like they did, but this was different. This was truly being under the spotlight.

I stepped up on the stage. Dell Johnson was reading the role of Death. He had a very mature look and a deep, resonant voice. He sang lead in the chorus and had been in three major musical productions at the school. None of the boys trying out deluded themselves. They were here to get some other role. Dell owned this one by his mere existence.

He looked at me and smiled as if my daring to challenge Iris was a childish act of bravado. It stirred heat under my breasts. I straightened my shoulders and closed my eyes for a moment, conjuring up the very scene Miss Hamilton had chosen to be read.

And then I began, reciting, illustrating I had memorized the lines as well. I could hear a very audible gasp of surprise and a stirring in the group. Dell, who I knew had intended just to read his lines without much feeling, suddenly found himself actually acting. Later, Miss Hamilton would tell me when someone is good, very good, it makes everyone else reach for his highest capability.

I looked at Dell. I moved toward him instinctively when the lines called for me to do so. I raised and lowered my voice, gazed into his eyes, drew him into the scene. We did so well together, we went beyond the pages we were given, and for a few seconds, no one, not even Miss Hamilton, realized it. Then she clapped her hands and we stopped.

"Well, thank you, Cinnamon. Thank you," she added with audible appreciation.

I glanced at Iris. She looked shocked, surprised, and angry at the same time, but that quickly turned to panic when she looked at Miss Hamilton and saw the depth of pleasure on her face. Then Iris turned back to me, long, glaring looks of envy delivered and redelivered as a series of visual slaps on my face. I walked off, feeling her eyes like two laser beams burning the back of my head. I ignored her and sat down to listen to the others, choosing whom I would select to play the various roles just to see how close I could come to what Miss Hamilton would do.

Surprisingly, I was nearly right about every one of them when I looked at the cast list posted the following morning. My name was prominent. I had won the part and that took over as the main topic of conversation in school. Most of my teachers congratulated me. Some looked genuinely surprised and impressed. Even Mr. Kaplan, the principal, stopped to wish me luck and encouragement. I was on pins and needles, anxious to rush out to the clinic to give Mommy the good news. Our first rehearsal was on Monday. Miss Hamilton assigned the pages to be memorized.

"I'm glad she chose you," Dell Johnson told me just before school ended. "I was afraid she wouldn't give you the chance."

"Thank you. Actually, she asked me to try out," I told him. That raised his eyebrows.

"Really?" He paused and looked around us to be sure what we said wouldn't be overheard. "You know, you'd better be careful about her," he advised.

"Why?"

"I've heard things, and I've got to warn you . . . Iris is pretty upset. She's already suggesting . . ." He rolled his eyes.

"Suggesting what?"

"Dirty stuff," he said. "Between you and Miss Hamilton," he added.

"She better not do it in front of me," I said.

"Don't worry, she won't. She doesn't work that way." He leaned toward me to add, "Just ignore them all, Cinnamon. Concentrate on the play. You'll be great," he said.

He sounded sincere, but I wondered if I could trust him. It was the beginning, I thought, the beginning of all the little intrigues that would surround and invade every dramatic project with which I would become involved. As always, the hardest part was acting in real life and the easiest thing was doing the actual performance. The line between the real and the imagined was blurred. Once again, I understood that life itself was an ongoing play.

Shakespeare was right: the world was a stage and all of us merely players.

Well, it was my time to play and, I was now determined, I would.

Mommy was so ecstatic over the news, I thought she might get up, ask for her clothes and walk out of the clinic with me right then and there.

"I knew you would be chosen, Cinnamon. She would have had to be a dullard not to see your talents," Mommy told me.

"Sometimes, talent isn't what determines who does and does not get the good roles, Mommy," I said. "You taught me that."

She stared at me a moment, her eyes darkening.

"Of course you're right, honey," she said. "But I never meant to cause you to be cynical at so young an age. We need our childhood faiths sometimes. We need to believe in magic and wonder and have pure, innocent hope. Otherwise, the world out there is a very dark, disappointing place and frankly, it's the only world we have."

"I believe in the magic, Mommy, but it's magic we make for ourselves. Those who trust and have too much faith suffer the most," I said.

What she didn't know was that I was talking about Daddy and how much faith and trust she had in him. How would she react when she found out about him? Would she crumble and end up back in here? I would hate him forever, I thought.

"You're right, Cinnamon. I just want you to find a good balance."

"I will," I promised.

She wanted me to read from the play script and talk about the part. She was determined to get better quickly now and be there to help me give the best possible performance.

"When are you coming home, Mommy? Has the doctor told you?"

"He wants me to stay a few more days, to grow stronger and to be sure I am all right," she said. "Daddy thinks that's best, too."

"Really?"

"Yes. He seems so troubled these days, so distant. I feel sorry for him, sorry for what all this has done to him," she said.

"Don't you feel that way, Mommy," I charged. I was a bit too adamant.

"Why not?"

"You're the one who's suffered! You had all the pain and all the disappointment, Mommy."

"Okay, honey. Let's try not to talk about me anymore. Let's concentrate on you for a while. I can't wait to see you on that stage. Read some more," she urged.

I softened my hard heart and did what she asked. In fact, the play soon became my whole life. I rushed through my homework at night and then went upstairs to the magic attic room to read and recite aloud. It just felt better to do it in that room, our room for stories and dreams. I soon memorized the whole play, everyone's part as well as my own. I could deliver my lines and then Dell's, actually assuming his position and lowering my voice to sound like him.

It felt so good. I was safe, wrapped in the cocoon of the imaginary world, the characters, the time and the place. I was no longer here in a house where sad tears streaked the walls, where dark shadows brushed away our smiles, where old voices full of disappointments and trouble echoed in the silences that hung in every corner during the hours when darkness draped over us and the moon fell victim to night's long thick clouds.

The play was the thing, my everything, my new world. It filled the void that had been dug and created the day I spied on Daddy and saw him kiss that strange woman on the lips. I had someplace to go to avoid him, something else to think about and fill my head, shoving out the anger and the disappointment that followed the memory of that dreadful moment. It helped me tolerate Grandmother Beverly, to flick off her nasty comments and criticism or let it float on by, unheard, unrecognized. When she began one of her lectures, I stared at her and in my mind, I rolled off lines from the play, listening to the voices in my head instead of her. In a way I had become just like Mommy, able to ignore her.

Perhaps most of all, the play loomed as the one big thing that would restore Mommy, bring her happiness and pleasure, help her to forget her tragedy and depression and bring us together in our special way once more.

And then, as if Grandmother Beverly understood all this, she honed in on her opportunity to ruin it, to shut another door and maybe drive Mommy back into despair. This opportunity came from the ugliest and nastiest of the rumors that girls like Iris Ainsley kept swarming like angry bees around me. She was so beautiful and intelligent. She had more than most girls dreamed of having, but her jealousy was too strong. It replaced the soft blue in her eyes with a putrid green and turned those perfect lips into writhing corkscrews, turning and twisting words and thoughts until they spilled out around me in the form of accusations about Miss Hamilton and myself.

The clouds steamed in from the north, cold and dark, eager to close off my sunshine.

I couldn't let it happen.

I wouldn't let it happen.

I drew strength from my spirits, my old pictures in the attic and the voices in the walls.

And I went forth to do battle with all the demons inside my home and out.

7

Bright Lights Can Burn

It really began when Miss Hamilton decided to hold small rehearsals at her house on weekends. Mommy had returned home from the clinic by then. The doctor had given her some medication to keep her calm. She was still weak, fragile, tired by early evening. When she came home and saw the changes Grandmother Beverly had made, she was very upset, but Daddy quickly reminded her that she had to remain tranquil and not get herself so worked up that she suffered a relapse. He promised to restore whatever she wished restored, but he took his time doing it, so I found her pictures in the basement myself and took down the ones Grandmother Beverly had put in their place. Mommy supervised the restoration while Grandmother Beverly fumed in the living room, staring at her television programs.

It was more difficult to restore the furniture in the living room and to reconstruct the kitchen. Mommy wasn't up to working yet, which meant Grandmother Beverly still prepared the meals. As long as she was doing that, she wanted the kitchen to be "sensible and organized." Mommy and I removed as many of the changes in her and Daddy's bedroom that we could. I found their previous window curtains and we rehung them. I had to go to the department store to buy bedding similar to what they had before Grandmother Beverly had replaced it. She had thrown Mommy's choices away.

Everything we did, Grandmother Beverly challenged and argued over, but we didn't pay any attention. As Mommy had decided, we nodded, said yes and then did what we wanted. It was beginning to be fun again.

I took Mommy for walks. Color returned to her cheeks. Her appetite grew better and I was more hopeful and happier than I had been in weeks. I waited to tell her about Clarence and what Grandmother Beverly had done. He phoned a few times, but each time, he sounded terrified of talking too long. We made vague promises to see each other as soon as possible, but I sensed that we each knew our plans were fantasies. I could feel him letting go of my hand.

I felt heartsick, but helpless. My first disappointment in love, I thought, would certainly not be my last. By the time I decided Mommy was strong enough to hear about the whole incident, I decided there wasn't any point in upsetting her over something that no longer mattered. We were too involved in my play by now anyway. That absorbed most of our time together. Mommy enjoyed playing different roles and rehearsing with me. We would do it in the living room sometimes, which drove Grandmother Beverly away. Often, we would stop and throw lines back and forth, even at dinner. It was truly as if we had set up that *fourth wall:* impenetrable and protective. Grandmother Beverly couldn't do anything but look in at us.

My first weekend rehearsal at Miss Hamilton's seemed innocent enough because Dell and two other members of the cast were there as well. We came in the morning and then she sent out for pizza and we had lunch before putting in another hour.

The weekend rehearsals were important and better because we were all fresh for them, not coming to a rehearsal after a full day of school. We had more time to analyze the lines, talk about our characters and think about our reactions.

Miss Hamilton had a small house. The living room wasn't much bigger than my parents' bedroom, but it was a comfortable two-story Queen Anne with a patch of lawn in front and a little backyard. The house itself was done in a Wedgwood blue cladding with black shutters. She had a patio at the rear of the house and a sunroom off the kitchen. We rehearsed in the living room, pushing aside some furniture to get a wide enough space for stage movements. I learned about blocking, moving upstage and downstage, projecting to the audience and reacting to characters. She at least knew all the basic things about theater, and she appreciated my interpretations and insights into my character. Most of that came from the sessions Mommy and I had spent together.

The third weekend Dell was unable to attend rehearsal because he was going on a trip with his family. I thought Miss Hamilton would just skip it, but she suggested I come over anyway. She said she would play his part and we would refine my performance. The play itself had been criticized as too adult, not something the student body would appreciate and support, but she stuck to her choice, defending it as a significant dramatic work.

"Besides," she reasoned, "our students get enough fluff on television and at the movies. They deserve something different for a change."

There was already some resentment toward her because of that. However, she saw it all as a greater challenge, "We have to win their respect, leave them in awe, show them what real talent can do," she told me. "You'll never forget this, Cinnamon. Everyone starts somewhere."

It both amused and intrigued me that she believed I could be a real actress and make a living at it, perhaps even become famous. Was I permitting her own frustrated dreams to move over into mine? I supposed there was only one way to find out for sure and that was to be on the stage when the curtain opened and when it finally closed.

The applause will tell, I told myself, as well as the afterward. Would people really remember my performance? Would they talk about it a day later? It was truly exciting. I couldn't help but do everything possible to make it work.

That third weekend, I was surprised when I arrived at Miss Hamilton's and discovered none of the other members of the cast would be there.

"We're just doing your big scenes," she explained. "I didn't see the point in bringing them all here this time."

I suppose I was aiding and abetting the gossipmongers and hatemongers in my school, but I couldn't help being nervous alone in Miss Hamilton's house. Dell had successfully planted the seeds of suspicion in the darkest, deepest places of my imagination.

"She's nearly thirty," he told me, "and no one has ever seen her with a man. Why doesn't she have a boyfriend at least? She's not that bad looking, is she?"

"I don't care," I told him. "Her personal life is her own, and besides, you and everyone else can't know what she does or who she sees out of school."

He shrugged.

"I'm just telling you what people say," he replied.

I hated that, the pretended indifference and innocence people put on when underneath they are enjoying the spreading of rumors. When I mentioned it to Mommy, she nodded and said, "Life for most people is so boring, they have to find ways to make it interesting, even if it means hurting someone. Watch out for that," she warned. "It's not only the jealous who do such things, Cinnamon. It's sometimes just people who literally have nothing better to do. Sometimes, I think they're the worst."

Miss Hamilton began our rehearsal the same way as before: reviewing where we were in the script and then starting a discussion of what we were about to rehearse.

"When you are alone with Death, you've got to keep the audience thinking you don't know who he really is. Think of him only as a charming, handsome man, so when you reveal the truth, that you've known all along, it will both shock and amaze the audience," she said.

I knew this, but I listened as if I didn't. Then we began our rehearsal with her reading Dell's lines.

"I know it's hard for you to look at me and think of me as a handsome young man," she said after a few minutes, "but that's what you have to do."

She paused when I looked skeptical. She thought a moment and said, "A friend of mine who is an actress told me she had to do a love scene with a man she not only didn't like, but whom she said had bad breath, even body odor. She said just the thought of doing it turned her stomach. She was in tears about it. She thought she would do so badly she would hurt her career forever."

"What happened?" I asked.

"An older actor gave her some good advice. He told her to imagine the man was someone she liked, someone she actually loved, if possible, and see only that person. If she concentrated hard enough, he told her, she wouldn't smell a thing. She said it worked and she got through the performance."

"Why didn't she just tell the man he stunk?" I asked.

Miss Hamilton smiled and tilted her head, the small dimple in her left cheek flashing in and out.

"Now, Cinnamon, how do you think that would have gone over? What sort of relationship would they have on the stage? He might pretend to appreciate her honesty, but don't you think his ego would have been bruised badly? Remember that essay we read about the messenger? He was despised more than the message."

"I guess when the truth is painful, it's better to turn to illusion," I said.

"Yes." She smiled. "But don't go telling people I advised you to tell lies," she warned and we both laughed.

We started rehearsing again. She wanted me

to keep eye contact, to look mesmerized by Death. She brought herself so close to me, to my lips, I felt my heart flutter in a panic. I think she saw it in my eyes finally and stopped.

She looked embarrassed for both of us.

"Well, let's take a short break. Would you like something to drink . . . tea, perhaps? It's always a good idea to have some tea and honey when you're on the stage."

"Fine," I said.

While I waited I looked about her living room. She had some pretty vases, some crystals on a shelf, inexpensive paintings of Paris, French villages, a seacoast scene that was somewhere in Italy. Were these places she had been or places she dreamed of visiting? What I realized was there were no pictures of family.

"Have you been to any of these places?" I asked nodding at the pictures when she returned with our cups of tea and some biscuits.

"Oh. No, but I will get there someday," she said. "Maybe even this summer. I've been saving."

"Where are you from, Miss Hamilton?"

"Well," she began setting the tray down and offering me my cup, "I'm from lots of places unfortunately."

"Why unfortunately? Was your father in the army or something?"

"No." She sipped her tea, looking at me over the cup for a moment as if she were deciding whether she should fall back on illusion or deal with the truth. She chose the truth. "I never knew my father, nor my mother."

"I don't understand," I said.

"I was an orphan, Cinnamon, then a foster child."

"Oh." I felt terrible asking personal questions now. "I'm sorry. I didn't mean to pry."

"It's all right. I think my being an orphan had a great deal to do with why I wanted to get into the theater first and then into teaching. When you're in a play, the whole cast becomes an extended family, especially if it has a long run. You're sometimes closer to your fellow actors than you are with your real family. At least, that's what they all used to tell me. Now I enjoy teaching, being close to my students, being a real part of their lives. Sometimes, I think I'm more involved, more concerned because I don't have a real family."

"Were you ever married?" I asked, nearly biting my own lower lip after asking.

She smiled again, sipped some tea, put her cup down and looked at me.

"You would think that nowadays people would be a lot more tolerant of women who weren't married or in a relationship by my age, but some ideas are branded in our social consciousness so deeply, we can't help being suspicious or critical of others who don't fit neatly in little boxes. Don't think I haven't been urged by older teachers and by administrators to settle down. As if it's my fault that Mr. Right hasn't come along," she added.

"I was almost married once, but in the end, we both decided it wouldn't have worked," she continued. "We were sensible and mature and lucky. Most people get involved too quickly these days and their relationships don't have the timber to last. Then, there's all that unfortunate business afterward . . . one or the other drifts away or things get unpleasant.

"You've got to really believe this is it for you. Maybe I'm more careful than most people because I never had a real parent-child relationship."

She paused and laughed.

"It's fun to be your own psychotherapist sometimes, but most of the time, I'd rather just let destiny unravel the spool called Ella Hamilton."

"Ella?"

"Yes," she said sipping her tea.

"Well if you had no mother or father, who named you?"

"Someone at the orphanage, I suppose. I never minded my name. It means a female possessing supernatural loveliness. How's that?"

"That's very nice."

"Actually, it's a name that fits you better than it does me, Cinnamon."

I didn't blush as much as feel a warmth travel up my neck, a warmth that made me shift my eyes from her.

"You've got to get used to people complimenting you, complimenting your unique look and your talents," she said seeing my discomfort. "I'm glad you're not like so many of your classmates. You're far more mature. You don't giggle after everything you say and you have self-confidence.

"I know you're frightened inside. Everyone is, but you cloak it well and you've already developed the ability to keep it under control. That's why I'm so convinced you're going to succeed on the stage," she continued.

I lifted my eyes and looked at her. Now that we had gotten to know each other better, I wanted to like her. I wanted to lower that wall between us. I wanted to trust her. Why couldn't we be friends, honest friends, innocent friends? Damn the rumors. If I wanted to give her a friendly hug, I would.

"Should we get back to work?" she asked.

"Yes," I said.

We began the scene again and I did what she advised. I didn't see her. I saw Dell's handsome face, heard his vibrant voice. We were inches apart and I was really getting into the role when suddenly, we were both surprised by a flash of light that bounced off the mirror above the mantel. We both turned toward the window facing the street.

"What was that?" I asked.

She shook her head.

"I don't know." She went to the window and gazed out. "No one's there."

She shrugged.

"Maybe a passing vehicle reflected sunlight."

"It's cloudy, Miss Hamilton." I went to the window and looked out, too. The street just seemed too quiet to me. "It was someone," I muttered.

"Well, whoever it was is gone. It doesn't really matter now," she said.

Little did she know.

She had more innocence and trust in her than I would have expected for someone with her background.

I came from a family. I had parents.

And yet I knew in my heart something terrible loomed just on the other side of that *fourth wall* we so lovingly cherished. Hard lessons would teach me that it was far from enough protection.

Like a second shoe, it dropped two days later at school. I had just arrived and was walking toward homeroom when I noticed a crowd around the general bulletin board placed at the center of the main corridor. Most of the students were laughing. The crowd began to grow larger. I approached slowly with a thudding heart, and when those on the perimeter of the clump saw me, they stepped aside, clearing an aisle for me to walk down as I approached the bulletin board.

There, too high up to reach without a stepladder, was a picture of Miss Hamilton and me at her home, in the rehearsal, just at the point where we were standing inches from each other, our lips so close it did look like we were about to kiss. The caption under the picture was in big block letters and read: TEACHER'S PET OR SOMETHING MORE?

"Who did that?" I screamed.

"We thought you did," Iris Ainsley quipped from the outside of the continually gathering group. Everyone laughed.

I turned on her. I was so crazed with hate, my whole body shook. Those between us saw it and stepped back.

"You disgusting, jealous little girl. You were spying on our rehearsal this Saturday. You were the one who took this picture and you know we were just rehearsing."

"Do you have to rehearse to do that?" someone else cracked. The group laughed again.

"Do what?" I cried, twisting a sarcastic smile and glaring back at Iris. "Try to ruin someone's reputation? No, she doesn't have to rehearse for that. She's spoiled rotten and vicious enough without any training. Go on and laugh, but if any one of you take something from the princess here, she'll do something just as cruel to you."

Some smiles wilted as they considered what I was suggesting.

"What's going on here?" we all heard Mr. Kaplan demand. He came toward us and the students split up quickly, heading toward their various homerooms. Iris hesitated a moment, smirked at me and left. I stood waiting for him.

"What's going on, Cinnamon?"

By now I was sure the color had left my cheeks. I know I felt sick and wanted to flee the place.

"Iris Ainsley or one of her friends took that picture of my rehearsal with Miss Hamilton and put it up there with that stupid caption," I said nodding at the board.

He looked up at it, widened his eyes and glanced at me.

"Go to your homeroom before you're late," he ordered. Then he went off to get the custodian to bring a ladder and take the picture and the caption down.

Damage, however, was done. Mr. Kaplan called Miss Hamilton to the office and showed the picture to her. The blood that I was sure had drained from her face at the sight of the photo and its caption remained absent from her complexion most of the day. She looked pale and weak and in great anguish. I felt so sorry for her, but I was afraid to show too much affection and concern. Everyone's eyes were on us, just waiting for us to comfort each other. But she didn't speak to me or to anyone else until rehearsal began after school.

"Most of you are quite aware of what went on this morning. Some disgusting-minded person did a very nasty thing. Because of it,

I've been asked not to hold any more weekend rehearsals at my home. I don't think it's going to hurt us. You're all too dedicated to this play to be set back, and I want you all to know how proud I am of the efforts you've made. We're going to show them," she declared.

Then she looked directly at me.

"If I've brought any of you any pain and trouble by not anticipating some of the disgusting things people can do, I apologize. I'll be a great deal more aware of the possibilities from now on, believe me.

"But I don't want this to color your enthusiasm with any gray. Let's work harder. Let's make this a success. Okay?"

"Absolutely," Dell cried. The rest of us applauded and the rehearsal began. Every time Miss Hamilton approached me or touched my arm, I could feel the self-consciousness seeping in. How I hated Iris Ainsley and her buffoons for doing this to us, but I couldn't let her win. I couldn't fall apart now.

It was more difficult than I anticipated because the picture was just a start. When I arrived home that day, I found that someone had called the house and given Grandmother Beverly an anonymous nasty message, which she quickly passed on to Mommy. She used the opportunity to tell her about the scene between Clarence and me in the attic and what she had done about it, warning Mommy that I was degenerating quickly and blaming it on Mommy's permissive attitude when it came to supervising me. Mommy looked devastated, weakened and pale by the time I arrived.

She was in her bedroom sitting in her soft chair, just waiting for me. The moment I saw her face, I knew what had happened.

"Did the principal call here?" I immediately asked.

"No, why would he call, honey?"

I told her about the picture, how it had happened and what some nasty, jealous students had done. She nodded as she listened and then began to tell me about her conversation with Grandmother Beverly.

"Why didn't you tell me anything about Clarence Baron, Cinnamon?"

"It was over and I didn't see why I should trouble you, especially since you had just come home from the clinic," I explained.

She nodded.

"But you should have told me by now, don't you think?"

"Maybe. I'm sorry."

"Your father hasn't mentioned it either. I'm sure he knows too, right?"

I looked up at her.

"No, I'm not so sure," I said. "Grandmother Beverly doesn't need reinforcements when she goes into battle."

"He's never spoken to you about it?" she asked.

I shook my head.

"How odd," she muttered and looked thoughtful. "Well, maybe you're right. She's such an overbearing woman. She thinks she's been ordained to run all our lives or something. But, I am troubled by all that's happened, honey. What did Miss Hamilton do today?"

"She ended our weekend rehearsals. I think the principal forced her to do that. She's really hurt. I felt worse for her than I did for myself."

"Yes. Sometimes, innuendo is enough, too much." Mommy looked at me. "There's not a shred of truth to the ugly stories, is there?"

I shook my head slowly, the tears coming hot and heavy into my eyes.

"How could you even ask?" I said.

"You're right," she replied quickly, "but you see what the power of suggestion can be? Even I was worried for a moment, Cinnamon. I shouldn't have been, but it's only natural, I suppose. I'm your mother. I have to worry."

"I hate them. I hate them so much," I said. "I wish I did have spiritual powers and could put a curse on all of them."

She smiled.

"They'll put a curse on themselves with their own actions. It might take a while, but those kind always end up eating out their own hearts, honey. Come here," she said and held out her arms.

I stepped forward and she hugged me tightly.

"I love you, Cinnamon. I trust you and I believe you."

"Thank you, Mommy," I said.

"What happened to Clarence?" she asked and I told her.

"You don't want to see him anymore?"

"I think he's moved on, Mommy. We were good friends and maybe we should have left it that way."

She nodded.

"I understand. More than you know," she added with a cryptic look in her eyes.

Either nothing was mentioned to Daddy, or if it was, he chose to ignore it. Grandmother Beverly made some veiled remarks at dinner, but Daddy seemed very distracted, lost in his own thoughts. Mommy noticed, too.

"Is something troubling you, Taylor?" She asked.

"What? No," he said quickly, far too quickly.

"You can't treat me like a thin-shelled egg forever," Mommy told him. "It will make me feel worse."

He gazed at Grandmother Beverly and then smiled at Mommy.

"It's just this market, with the Feds making everyone nervous threatening to raise rates, not to raise rates," he explained. "Some of my clients are driving me bonkers."

"I wish you thought about getting yourself into something else, Taylor. You used to talk about establishing your own financial group for estate investments instead of doing battle daily in that madhouse called the stock market."

He nodded.

"Maybe soon," he said.

Grandmother Beverly made a small, throaty sound of skepticism and then nodded to me to start clearing away the dishes.

Mommy glanced at me and I at her. We were spiritual sisters. We shared a sensitivity that told us something wasn't quite right. I had my own ideas about it, of course, and I made the mistake of looking away too quickly. Later that evening, Mommy called me into her bedroom.

"Is there something you know, you all know, that Daddy doesn't want to tell me, Cinnamon?"

I shook my head. How could I ever tell her what I had seen?

"You know, worrying about something terrible happening can make you almost as sick as the terrible thing itself," she said.

I nodded, but kept my eyes down. I felt so trapped.

"All right, honey. I don't want you to worry either. You have too much on your mind these days with your schoolwork, your tests and the play coming up. Let's just think about the good things," she suggested.

I smiled and nodded.

"Okay, Mommy."

The week before the play was so intense. We had three evening dress rehearsals in a row so the lighting, the sets, the props and, of course, our performances could be sharpened and coordinated. We made so many mistakes, I was convinced it would be a total disaster. People like Iris Ainsley would get what they wanted, their sweet, vicious revenge. It might very well destroy Miss Hamilton's career as well, I thought. What terrible thing had I done when I took this role and assumed this awesome responsibility?

Miss Hamilton tried to assure us that blunders during dress rehearsals were a good thing.

"Let's make all our mistakes these nights and be perfect in front of the audience," she said.

The evening before the play opened, I had a nightmare that I had lost my voice. When I stepped onto the stage, I couldn't make a sound and the whole audience broke into a fit of hysterical laughter. I saw Iris's face burst into a fat, happy smile and Mommy's face streaked with tears. I woke and found my heart was pounding. It seemed impossible to fall back to sleep and that made me even more nervous. If I'm not rested and I'm exhausted, I'll forget lines, moves, everything. When the alarm sounded in the morning, I woke in a panic. My eyes looked bloodshot. I wanted to stay home, but I knew if I didn't attend school, the principal could keep me from performing.

Mommy rose to have breakfast with me and encourage me.

"I know this is a big day for you. You'll be floating, hardly hearing or seeing anything, Cinnamon, but you've just got to stay firm, stay confident. You'll be wonderful," she assured me.

Here she was recently recovered from a terrible emotional crisis in her life giving me comfort and boosting my morale. How I loved her, I thought, and hugged her tightly before I left for school. She was right about the day. It seemed to take forever. I spent most of my class time glancing at the clock, longing for the sound of the bell, hardly hearing the teachers. Thankfully, none had scheduled an exam. In the cafeteria I sat with members of the cast. We had gravitated to each other out of a mutual sense of anxiety, drawing comfort from each of us freely admitting he or she had trouble sleeping the night before, and everyone confessing fear of forgetting lines.

"Don't worry about it," Dell assured us. "When you step onto that stage tonight, you won't remember being afraid and you won't be tired. You'll be so juiced."

I didn't see how that was possible. When school finally ended, Miss Hamilton stopped me in the hallway and told me to just go home and rest. We had an early call for makeup and then it would begin.

Or end.

At home Mommy had gotten herself back into the flow of activity. She took over preparing our dinner because she wanted to be sure I ate something light. Daddy had promised to get home early. Grandmother Beverly was coming to the play, too, "to see if all this time had been wasted."

Mommy looked so much her old self, hovering around me as I prepared to leave for the school theater. All I could think was if I failed, she might regress. It added to the pressure.

"You'll do fine, honey," she told me as I started down the stairs. "Just being part of something like this is wonderful. You'll see."

We hugged. Daddy was still not home, but he had called to say he was on his way. Miriam Levy, the head of our student makeup crew, was coming by to pick me up. I headed out, looking back once to wave to Mommy in the doorway, and then I released a hot, anxious breath and got into Miriam's car.

There was so much commotion in the makeup room, it was hard to worry. Miss Hamilton was busy with details, putting out small fires. We had no time to talk. Finally, twenty minutes before the opening curtain, she gathered the cast together and gave us her pep talk.

"I want you all to know that I'm proud of you already. In my short life in the theater, I learned that what makes the difference is not perfection, but the ability to deal with imperfection. Mistakes will happen. Expect them, but stay on your feet and react to them so that the audience never knows. Good luck, gang. Thanks for giving me so much of yourselves," she concluded, her eyes fixed solely on me.

We took our positions. Someone cried, "The place is full!"

My heart dipped like a yo-yo in my chest and touched the bottom of my stomach. I thought I would vomit and was happy Mommy had made sure I had a very light dinner. When the curtain opened, there was applause for the set and it began.

Like a baby duckling just realizing it can swim, I glided through the lights. I could feel myself growing stronger, more confident with every successful line delivered. Dell was as strong as ever — even stronger — and our performances enhanced each other's. I felt as if I had been on the stage all my life. Maybe it was remembering Mommy and myself in the attic, all those stories we acted, those people I portrayed. Whatever, I didn't miss a word or fail to hit my marks.

When it came time for Dell's and my most dramatic scene, I could sense that the audience was rapt, but I didn't think of them. I thought of who I was in the play and what I was saying and what was happening. How much I wanted the sense of calm and completion my character had at this moment. How brave her love had made her. The sweet tragedy brought tears and when the final curtain closed, the applause was thunderous.

I had avoided looking directly at the audience all evening. The lights had helped block them out, but when we took our curtain calls, and I came out on the stage, I was overwhelmed by the sight of all those people rising to their feet. I glanced at Miss Hamilton. She was glowing so brightly, she looked like a little girl again.

The moment I stepped off the stage, we hugged.

"Thank you," I told her.

"No, Cinnamon, thank you. Thank you for being who I thought you were. This is just the beginning for you," she promised.

Afterward, friends and family came backstage. Mommy looked so beautiful and so healthy, my heart burst for joy. Daddy couldn't stop complimenting me and I saw how much he enjoyed the accolades other people were lavishing on him.

"She's a natural."

"What a talented young lady."

"You must be so proud."

In the background, looking overwhelmed herself, stood Grandmother Beverly. She, too, welcomed the praise and was glad to take credit for being a member of my family.

"I knew you would do well, honey," Mommy whispered. "Our spirits assured me.

"And you know what?" she added.

"What?"

"They were here, too. I could hear them clapping for you."

We laughed.

Was the world really this wonderful after all?

8

My Turn to Shine

"There's someone I'd like you to meet," Miss Hamilton told me when the crowd began to thin out.

Mommy, Daddy and Grandmother Beverly had left while I cleaned off my makeup and changed. They were waiting in the lobby. I turned from the makeup mirror and looked up at a tall, thin man with small dark eyes, a sharp straight nose and a square-boned, cleft chin. He had thin, arrogant lips and styled dark brown hair. He looked impeccably dressed in a gray, pin-striped suit and tie. There was a small twist in the right corner of his mouth that made him look lofty, condescending.

"Cinnamon, I'd like you to meet a good friend of mine, Edmond Senetsky."

"Hello," I said, gazing quizzically at Miss Hamilton. It was obvious to me from the way she was gloating that this man was important to her.

He extended his right hand, a slim hand with long fingers, one of which was dressed in a gold and diamond band. It wasn't a wedding ring, just a very expensive piece of jewelry.

I stood up quickly and shook his hand. He had a soft, unremarkable grip, more like the grip of someone just letting go.

"Edmond is a theatrical agent, Cinnamon. I once had illusions of him representing me," Miss Hamilton said. She laughed, but he didn't.

"I think the worst thing you can do to someone is give them false hope," he declared firmly. He looked at Miss Hamilton and added, "Those who can, do; and those who can't, teach."

She didn't stop smiling, but I thought that was a mean thing to say and stopped smiling at him.

"He's right, Cinnamon," Miss Hamilton said quickly. "There's no disgrace in being the teacher either. You get to live on through your students."

"Precisely," Edmond said. He wasn't English, but he tried to speak so perfectly, he sounded like someone imitating a distinguished Englishman.

"Anyway, honey, you might have heard me mention Edmond's mother, Madame Senetsky who was once a very famous Russian stage actress and who now operates one of the most prestigious dramatic arts schools on the East coast. Actually, she takes on only a handful of new students every year. Edmond thinks you could be one of them."

"I didn't say that exactly," he corrected

quickly, showing some annoyance. "You've given a passable performance tonight for a high-school girl."

"Passable, Edmond?" Miss Hamilton pushed.

"Well, perhaps somewhat more remarkable than that, but I must warn you, the *crème de la crème* auditions for my mother every year. It's one thing to compete with your classmates in a school this size, but quite another to go head to head against the best in the country."

"You're going to frighten her away, Edmond," Miss Hamilton told him.

"If I do, she's meant to be away," he said. He drew a step closer to me. His eyes were beady, his lashes long enough to make any girl green with envy. "Let me tell you this one truth about the theater, the movies, television, modeling, anything that has to do with performance, Miss . . ."

"Cinnamon," Miss Hamilton said. "Cinnamon Carlson."

"Yes, Cinnamon. All of it is at least thirty percent perseverance. Then there is about thirty percent luck, being in the right place at the right time. The rest has to do with talent. If it's in you to do it, you'll do it, if not . . ."

"I'll teach?" I countered.

Miss Hamilton laughed.

"Or take tickets at the entrance," he shot back. He turned to Miss Hamilton. "You will have the information you need." He looked at me. "Good luck."

"That's thirty percent," I said.

He almost smiled. His eyes brightened with some appreciation. Then he nodded, thanked Miss Hamilton for inviting him and left.

"Who *was* that?" I grimaced.

"He really is a very powerful agent, Cinnamon, and his mother's school is really the most sought after in the country. All her graduates go on to find success in a most competitive world. I want you to think about auditioning. Two weeks from now, in New York. I'll go with you, if you like. I'll get all the information to you and your parents."

"I don't know, Miss Hamilton."

"Talk it over with your family. I'll mention it to your mother and father when I see them out in the lobby now. You were wonderful, Cinnamon. Really wonderful."

She left me wondering what all this meant. Most of my fellow students were already planning their futures and applying to colleges. Daddy wanted me to go to his alma mater, NYU, but I had yet to submit the application. I was anxious to see how Mommy reacted to Miss Hamilton's suggestion.

By the time I arrived in the lobby, there were only a few stragglers left. Mommy and Daddy and Grandmother Beverly, who looked impatient, were still talking with Miss Hamilton.

"Here's our little star," Daddy said and gave me a kiss on the cheek. "We're all very proud of you, Cinnamon, very proud."

Miss Hamilton stood there, beaming. However, I saw how Grandmother Beverly was looking at her, her eyes fixed with accusations.

"I'm tired," I declared.

"Of course, you are, sweetheart," Mommy said. She put her arm around my shoulders. I said good night to Miss Hamilton and we left, my triumph hovering around me like an angelic light. Anyone left in the lobby and in the parking lot shouted their congratulations. I couldn't help but wonder where Iris Ainsely and her friends had gone to pout.

"Miss Hamilton told me about Edmond Senetsky," Mommy said after we started away. She and I sat in the rear and Grandmother Beverly sat up front because she hated sitting in the back. She said it made her feel like she was in a taxicab. I wondered why it didn't make her feel like she was in a limousine, but her answer was she hated that feeling, too.

"We'll have to learn more about this school," Daddy admonished.

"Ridiculous," Grandmother Beverly said. "What kind of an education will she get in a school run by an old woman?"

"She's not just an old woman. She's a famous international actress," I said.

"It sounds very exciting," Mommy declared.

"It's very competitive, Mommy. I don't see how I can get chosen."

"Of course you will," Mommy decided.

"Look what you did tonight."

"We'll see. It does sound very, very competitive," Daddy said, punctuating the air with a heavy note of caution. He glanced at Grandmother Beverly who simply shook her head and stared at the road.

I suddenly felt like the two of them were coconspirators, conspiring against Mommy's dreams and mine. My pride rose quickly up my spine like some flag of defiance.

"I'd like to try nevertheless," I announced, almost more out of spite than desire.

"Good," Mommy squealed and hugged me. "I'm so terribly proud of you, sweetheart, so very, very proud."

Dare I say I was proud of myself, too? Or was that being arrogant?

I didn't have to say it. Mommy could see it in my face. She was the only one who could, but that was enough, I thought. That was enough.

The next evening our second performance went as well as the first. During the curtain call, the president of the student government came up to present me with a bouquet of red and white roses. The audience was on its feet applauding. Mommy and Daddy had come again, but Grandmother Beverly had remained at home to watch one of her old movies.

When I arrived at school on Monday, the accolades continued. All of my teachers lavished so much praise on me, I felt myself in a constant blush. Iris Ainsley was never so quiet and in the background. She and her friends were chased off like mice into the corner of the cafeteria, whispering among themselves. They looked small and so insignificant, I chastised myself for ever taking them seriously enough to feel bad after anything they had said or done.

The cast remained close. We ate lunch together and all of us basked in the continuing adulation. Then, on Wednesday, Miss Hamilton gave me the information about the audition. It was being held in a week at a small off-Broadway theater Madame Senetsky used every year for this purpose. I clutched the paper containing the details in my hand. My parents had to call to make the appointment.

"If you want me to go with you, I will," Miss Hamilton offered again. "But it might be something you and your parents should do together, a family thing," she added. "I don't mean to interfere."

"I'm sure my mother would want you to go if I go," I said.

"Give it a try, Cinnamon. If you don't, you'll always wonder. Believe me. Those kinds of questions haunt you for your whole life."

I nodded, but I was so nervous about it that I almost decided not to tell Mommy when I arrived home that afternoon. She was reading and listening to music in her room, but I could tell from the way she sat and from the tightness of the lines in her face that she was upset about something. Was it something Grandmother

Beverly had done or said? I wondered.

"Hi, honey," she said lowering her book.

"What's wrong, Mommy?" I asked immediately. Her face was a book I could easily read.

She smiled at me.

"We're too alike, you and I. How can I ever hide anything? Your father was supposed to take us out to dinner, to celebrate your success, but he called just a half hour ago to tell me he was called to a very important meeting and wouldn't be home until ten tonight. Grandmother Beverly made one of her famous bland meat loafs."

My heart raced, chased my own rage.

"Let's go out for pizza," I suggested.

"Really?"

"Yes, Mommy. I'll change into something more pizza-ish and we'll just go ourselves," I said, my voice laced with defiance. She laughed.

"Yes, why not? Grandmother Beverly doesn't mind eating alone. She's alone when she's eating with us anyway," Mommy said.

We laughed and I went to change. Mommy informed Grandmother Beverly of our intentions.

"She didn't say a word," Mommy told me when we got into my car and I started for my favorite pizza hangout. "She barely nodded."

"She uses silence like a sword," I said.

"I can't help feeling sorry for her sometimes, Cinnamon. She has no real friends, no one from her past life with Grandpa Carlson who cares to stay in touch with her, just a bunch of busy-bodies looking for juicy gossip. She puts so much emphasis on taking care of Daddy and competing with me that she doesn't have time to nurture relationships. But the truth is your father seems oblivious to the both of us these days," she added sadly.

Should I tell her what I knew, what I had seen? Was she ready, strong enough? What if it set her back, wounded her so deeply she had to return to the clinic? How could I live with myself? How could I ever look at Daddy, much less live with him afterward? It was hard enough doing it now.

I swallowed the story back and stuffed it tightly in the dark drawer under my heart.

Mommy loved the pizza place. She said it reminded her so much of her own childhood and teenage years. She talked incessantly, almost with a nervous energy that made me suspicious, but she did tell me stories about her youth that I had never heard, stories about boyfriends and girlfriends and her own fantasies.

"I didn't want to be an actress. I wanted to be a singer. I had an old aunt, Grandma Gussie's sister Ethel who told me that you could train your voice or turn it into a good singing voice if you found a place where you could get a good echo. I found one about a half-mile from our house, a little canyon, and I used to go there and practice the scales. I think

I frightened off not only the birds and squirrels, but the insects. I did go out for chorus, but I was never chosen to do anything more than sing along.

"Fantasies die slow, quiet deaths. They're like cherry blossoms breaking away and sailing down slowly, still holding onto their color and their softness and beauty, but ending up on the ground to be blown about by cold winds.

"Don't let that happen to your dream, Cinnamon," she warned. "This is more than a fantasy. You've got something, a gift; and don't let anyone or anything stop you. Promise me. Promise me you won't let anyone discourage you," she begged.

I promised and then I showed her the paper Miss Hamilton had given me.

"Then this is real, an opportunity!" she cried. She was happier for me than I was for myself, I think. I hated myself for even harboring a hesitation. "I'll take care of this in the morning."

"Miss Hamilton offered to go with us if we'd like her to," I said.

Mommy seemed to lose some of her excitement and glow. I shouldn't have told her, I thought.

"Of course, if you'd like her to go with us, she can."

"It's not that important, Mommy. I think she's just so excited for me. She's an orphan, you know."

"Oh?"

We both ate some pizza and I told her as much as I knew about Miss Hamilton.

"No," Mommy decided after she heard the details, "she should go with us. She is the one really responsible for all this. Why shouldn't we make her part of it? Besides, if I treat her like I believed those nasty rumors, I would be as guilty as someone spreading them."

I nodded.

Then we went back to giggling, eating our pizza, listening to the music and acting like a couple of teenage sisters. It turned out to be the best time we had together since she had come back from the clinic.

When we got back to the house, I went to do my homework and study for a math test. Mommy returned to her reading. Daddy didn't come home at ten. It was nearly eleven-thirty when I heard his footsteps on the stairway. He went by my room quickly and quietly. I heard their bedroom door close and then the silence of sadness closed in around me, driving me to the sanctity of sleep.

The next day Mommy had all sorts of information for me when I returned from school. Madame Senetsky's administrative assistant told Mommy to have me prepare a speech from *The Taming of the Shrew.* We had a collection of Shakespearean plays and Mommy had already found the pages.

"We're going Saturday," she told me. "Ten A.M."

"Saturday! That's only two days away!"

"Don't worry. We'll practice plenty," she declared. Then she added, "Tell Miss Hamilton and ask her for any suggestions, too."

Meanwhile, Mommy and I began that evening. She thought it would be so right for me to practice in our attic room where my dramatic life had really had its beginning.

"Besides," she said almost in a whisper, "the spirits will be with us as they were with you on that stage."

Who was I to doubt it? I thought.

We went up right after dinner. Daddy came to see what we were doing because we were there so long. He listened a little and then he left, shaking his head and smiling. At dinner Friday night, Grandmother Beverly gave voice to her disapproval.

"Why shouldn't she be chosen?" she asked. "Don't believe all that business about it being very competitive. I saw that paper. I saw how expensive it is to attend that so-called school of dramatics. It's a waste of good money — and while she should be at a proper school learning something useful."

"It is expensive," Mommy agreed. I looked up quickly. Daddy stopped eating, too. "I was going to ask you to release some of the trust fund that Grandfather Carlson and you established for her."

"She's not to touch that until she's twenty-one," Grandmother Beverly declared.

"I know, but that wasn't well thought out. Young people need college money and they need that before they're twenty-one."

"But this isn't a college. It's . . . it's . . . a foolish indulgence. I won't agree to waste a cent on such nonsense."

"It is a hefty tuition," Daddy said softly.

"Yes, but it includes everything. She lives at the school, is taken under wing by Madame Senetsky."

"Lives at the school," Grandmother Beverly practically spit. "It's just some old New York house. She's running this scam to meet her expenses because she was probably a great failure."

"That's a lie," I cried. "I read all about her. She was a very famous actress and people from everywhere try to get into her school. I probably won't even have a chance."

"Lucky for you," Grandmother Beverly said.

Mommy looked like she was going to burst a blood vessel.

"Yes," I said calmly, softly, almost sweetly, "if I don't make it, it's probably lucky because I won't chase a foolish dream. You're so right, Grandmother Beverly."

Mommy's eyebrows went up and then she looked at me and I at her and we both burst into a fit of laughter that surprised Daddy and drove Grandmother Beverly from the table mumbling to herself.

Daddy woke up with a terrible sinus headache on Saturday morning. He had said he was going with us and would take us all to a nice lunch in Greenwich Village, but Mommy told him to stay home and nurse his head cold instead.

"You'll only be uncomfortable and take Cinnamon's attention from her work," Mommy added.

He didn't put up a great deal of resistance and, of course, Grandmother Beverly agreed.

"You should all stay home," she said.

"You don't want to come then?" Mommy asked her. "We could have a nice day in the city."

"Me? I hate the city," she replied, but she looked unsure of Mommy's motives, almost as if she wanted to believe we really hoped she would come. For the first time I wondered if Mommy was right about her: she was just a very lonely old woman we should pity.

We left and picked up Miss Hamilton. On the way in she talked about the auditions she had undergone during her acting days.

"Everyone is nervous. If you're not, you just don't care enough," she said.

"That's very true," Mommy agreed. "I imagine if you're too nonchalant, you give off an air of indifference and turn off the director."

"The trick, if there is a trick, is to not think of yourself in that theater on that small stage, Cinnamon. Get into the play. You know it so well. We read it in class earlier this year," she told Mommy.

"Yes, Cinnamon loved it, and actually went around reciting some of Kate's lines long before this."

"That's wonderful," Miss Hamilton said. "Then this is meant to be."

They got into a discussion about plays they had seen and by the time we arrived at the little theater, they were laughing and joking together like old friends. It made me happy and took away some of my nervousness, but I was still so terrified, I thought my legs would surely fold up beneath me the moment I stepped onto that stage.

When we entered the theater, we were surprised to see no other candidates. The room itself was dark and there was just a small spotlight turned on, dropping a circle of light upstage.

"Edmond told me this might be the case," Miss Hamilton whispered. "She doesn't like other candidates sitting around, watching someone else audition."

"Someone else?" Mommy said. "There's no one here at all!"

"Not true," we heard a strong, deep female voice state.

At the rear of the auditorium, seated in the shadows so that we could barely make her out was who we imagined to be Madame Senetsky herself. Her pewter gray hair was pulled tightly up into a coiled chignon at the top of her head and clipped with a large, black comb.

"Madame Senetsky?" Miss Hamilton asked.

"Of course. Please have your candidate take the stage immediately. Promptness is essential in the theater, as it should be in life itself," she added.

"Why is she sitting in the dark?" Mommy wondered in a whisper.

"Go on, Cinnamon," Miss Hamilton said. She moved into an aisle, taking the second seat and leaving the aisle seat for Mommy.

"She could greet us at least," Mommy muttered but sat.

I started for the stage, my heart not pounding or thumping so much as it was tightening in my chest. It felt difficult to breathe. Why should I be so nervous? I wondered. There's only one person in this audience, I told myself. It's not like it was at the school play with nearly a thousand in attendance. One pair of eyes and one pair of ears are out there.

Mommy was right. Why didn't she have the decency to greet us and at least make me feel comfortable? What arrogance, I thought. I grew angrier with every step toward the stage.

Who does she think she is? She didn't win an Academy Award, did she? Most people won't remember who she is. It's impolite not to have greeted Mommy and Miss Hamilton. I felt like turning around and unleashing a tirade that would shake that chignon loose.

Instead, I stepped onto the stage, took a deep breath, closed my eyes and told myself to be Kate, to move forward into the play, to do such a good job, I would make that pompous woman feel terrible about her treatment of us.

"Well?" she cried.

If that was intended to throw me off, to unnerve me and see whether I would crack and run off the stage, it didn't work.

"Well, indeed," I whispered.

I stepped forward and began . . .

"Fie, fie . . ."

I loved Kate, loved her fury and her defiance, but I also loved the way she was conquered, convinced and ultimately wooed to love Petruchio. In the end they were the most romantic, loving and considerate couple on earth. I dreamed I would have such a romance someday and such a marriage.

Miss Hamilton and Mommy clapped at the end of my speech. I stood there waiting to hear something, but there was just silence after that.

Then the spotlight went out.

"What the . . ."

There was just enough light from the aisle lamps for me to make my way back to them and for us to find our way to the exit doors. When we looked for Madame Senetsky, we saw no one.

"I don't understand," Mommy said. "Where is she? What are we supposed to do now?"

Miss Hamilton shook her head.

"I don't know any more than you do. I'm sorry."

"This is a ridiculous way to treat people. Who does she think she is?" Mommy cried. "Hello! Anyone here?"

We waited a moment and then Mommy said, "Let's get out of here."

We stepped out in the bright sunlight, all of us squinting.

"You were wonderful, Cinnamon," Mommy said. "If that woman had any insight, she would see it."

"Yes, you did great," Miss Hamilton said. "I'll call Edmond."

"Don't bother to waste your time and money," Mommy said. "She must be some kind of a nut or sadist. Let's have some lunch," she added, "and enjoy the rest of the day."

We did enjoy it. In the restaurant Mommy did an imitation of Madame Senetsky sitting in the rear of the theater. She seized her hair and pulled it up so tightly, her eyelids stretched. Miss Hamilton and I laughed. I knew the both of them were trying to make me feel better and I appreciated their efforts and pretended not to be bothered.

But I had left that theater feeling so exposed, so embarrassed. It was as if a doctor had asked me to undress and then left me naked in the examination room.

On the way home, Mommy and I decided we wouldn't tell Grandmother Beverly anything. If we did, she would just gloat and chant how right she was about such schools and why it was a great waste of time and money. We told Daddy I performed well and we'd see, but I had no hope. He wasn't feeling much better and went to sleep early that evening.

The next day Miss Hamilton called to tell me she had phoned Edmond Senetsky and he had told her that was the way his mother conducted her auditions. She didn't have the patience for small talk and she didn't see the point of conversation before or after the audition. The audition was all that mattered to her. As to my chances, he repeated his admonition that there were dozens of candidates parading past her this week. She had seen six the day I was there, in fact.

Early the following week, I completed my application to NYU and to some state schools the guidance counselor had recommended for me. I was busy studying for tests. Acting began to drift back toward that place reserved for fantasies and dreams in my mind. Every day I entered her class, Miss Hamilton's eyes widened a bit in anticipation, but one look at my face told her I had no news, and soon she stopped anticipating any.

In the end Grandmother Beverly was probably right, I told myself. Just because she said everything in a hard, cold manner didn't mean it wasn't couched in truth. The thing is it was harder to accept reality when someone like

Grandmother Beverly, unhappy with reality herself, presented it to you or forced it on you. What did she dream about now? I wondered. When she laid her head upon her pillow and closed her eyes, what helped her sleep? What were her secret wishes and hopes? Or was her head always full of warnings and skepticism, turmoil spiraling forever behind her closed eyelids?

"Pity her," Mommy kept telling me now. It was as though her bout with her own demon and trouble had made her a far more compassionate person, full of little mercies instead of little terrors. In my heart of hearts, I thought she might even pity Daddy if she knew what I knew.

She still suspected something. He was more distant with every passing day. I feared the coming of his confessions and what it would bring down on this fragile house and family.

And then the letter came, the letter that would force so much truth upon us we would nearly drown. Mommy was waiting for me in the living room with it when I came home from school. She called to me and she held it out, unopened.

"It's come," she said.

"Why didn't you open it?" I asked taking it from her.

"It's yours, honey, yours to open."

I tore the envelope and pulled out the papers. The letter was so dripping with presumption and arrogance that I was sure it had either been written or directly dictated by Madame Senetsky herself.

Dear Ms Carlson:

You are to report to the Senetsky School of Performing Arts on July 7 at 10 A.M.

All tuition costs must be paid at that time.

Below is a list of required clothing and attached is a list of rules to follow while you are residing at the school. Any violation of any rule, no matter how small or insignificant it might appear, will result in expulsion and the forfeiture of tuition paid.

The contract is included and must be signed and returned by a parent or legal guardian within two working days of receipt of this letter.

Yours truly,
Madame Senetsky

I handed it to Mommy and she read it quickly, burst into laughter and then stopped abruptly and considered.

"I don't know if she's a madwoman or what. She treats us like nothing and then accepts you."

"What should I do?"

"Well, you'll go, of course. It's what you wanted, isn't it?"

I shook my head.

"I don't know. I'm so confused."

"Of course you'll go, honey. This is a great opportunity."

I went right to the phone and called Miss Hamilton. She was so happy, she started to cry. I told Mommy and she cried, too. All of us were crying and it was supposed to be a happy, wonderful moment.

A few minutes later, we heard the front door open and stepped out to greet Daddy.

"What's up?" he asked.

Mommy handed him the letter.

Daddy's expression as he read the letter and immediately afterward told me he was not only not expecting it, he was hoping it would never come. His low-keyed, "This is nice," took Mommy by surprise, too.

"Nice?" she countered. "Nice is all you can say?"

He glanced at me and then forced a smile.

"Well, I mean it's nice to have options, to be wanted in many places."

"Options? This isn't the stock market, Taylor. It's your daughter's future," Mommy snapped.

He nodded. I never saw him look this uncomfortable, not even in the mental clinic.

"I know that. I'm referring to all the choices she can have. It takes some thinking. You want to be sure you make the right decisions for yourself, Cinnamon," he told me. "Let's review it all, consider everything. That's all I'm saying," he told Mommy.

She smirked and stepped back.

"You've been listening to your mother too much, Taylor."

"Well, she's not all wrong. I bet if you looked into it, Cinnamon, you'd discover that most successful actors nowadays started at something else first. It's a very difficult, challenging thing and you might be better off attending a regular state university or something and getting a well-rounded education. While you did that, there would be nothing to stop you from going out for the plays and building experiences, right? Then, if you were still inclined to pursue it, you could audition again," he said as if it was as simple as fastening a seat belt.

Mommy shook her head.

"Why are you saying these things now, Taylor? Why didn't you say them when Miss Hamilton told us about the performing arts school? Why didn't you say them before we took her to the audition? Why didn't you say them all these days that have gone by since?"

Daddy looked pained.

"From what you told me about it, I have to admit, I never expected this," he said holding up the letter.

Mommy plucked it from his fingers.

"You should have had more faith," she said and turned away from him. "I'm getting dinner together. Your mother hasn't come back from the dentist yet."

"Oh? I thought she had a four o'clock appointment. She should have been back by now."

"Maybe she's shopping for a new bedroom set for us," Mommy muttered and walked off.

I stared at Daddy. His shoulders sagged, there were heavier bags under his eyes and he looked tired and pale. I didn't want to feel sorry for him, but I couldn't help it. He glanced at me and saw something different in my eyes. It made him look twice.

"I'm sorry if I upset you with my suggestions, Cinnamon. And it's not something Grand-mother put into my head. It's only meant to be sensible."

He started up the stairs, lifting his legs as if each weighed as much as his whole body. I saw him take a deep breath at the top and then continue toward his bedroom. I turned to go to the kitchen to help Mommy with dinner, but just as I did, I heard a loud thump from above. For a moment, I just stood there, lis-tening. Then Mommy came back into the hallway.

"What was that?" she asked.

I shook my head and lunged for the stairway. When I reached the top, I saw my father on the floor, lying on his side. His right leg twitched as he struggled to get up.

"Daddy!" I screamed and ran to him. Sec-onds later, Mommy was at my side.

His eyelids fluttered.

"What is it, Taylor? What happened?" Mommy asked him.

"Got dizzy," he said. He tried to rise again

and grimaced. "Pain," he said touching his chest.

"Don't move, Taylor. Don't try to get up. I'm calling for help. Stay with him, Cinnamon," Mommy told me and hurried to the phone in their bedroom.

I lowered Daddy's head gently to my lap. His lips looked blue, but he kept his eyes on me and forced a smile.

"It's all right," he said so low I could barely hear him. "I'll be all right."

I could barely see him through the glaze of tears on my eyes.

"Listen," he said. He beckoned me closer.

I leaned as far as I could.

"I'm sorry about all I said. I'm proud of you, proud they want you. It was the cost, but we'll find a way," he promised. He closed his eyes.

"The paramedics are on their way," Mommy cried coming from the bedroom. "How is he?"

"I don't know," I said.

She knelt beside him.

"Taylor, I'm here. I'm with you," she said grabbing his hand and holding it with both of hers. She wiped strands of hair from his forehead. His eyelids fluttered and then opened.

"Sorry," he said.

I couldn't help but wonder what his apology included.

Epilogue

Daddy didn't die, but he was diagnosed with a heart problem serious enough to require a pacemaker. Grandmother Beverly blamed his condition on Mommy, of course. She didn't come right out and say it, but she dropped her hints around the house like rat poison.

"It's no surprise," she remarked when the diagnosis was made. "Not with all he's had on his mind these days."

"Any man who carried his burdens would have dropped dead long ago."

"He was always a healthy man, but ever since I moved in here, I've seen him dwindling, eaten away."

Finally, one night before Daddy came home, Mommy was the one who dropped her fork on the plate and turned to Grandmother Beverly with critical eyes after she made another one of these remarks.

"Beverly," she said. I knew something hard was going to follow because she rarely called her Beverly. "I think you should seriously consider moving out of here, finding your own little place."

"What? You can't be serious," Grandmother Beverly said smiling. "Why, you need me more than ever around here now."

"I need you less than ever," Mommy retorted. "We need our own lives, without any interference and certainly without any static. You don't like this house and you are not happy living here. Because you're not happy, you do everything to make everyone else miserable.

"Maybe if you're living somewhere more to your liking, you'll be more satisfied. We'll have you for dinner often, of course, and you can visit whenever you like."

Grandmother Beverly nodded.

"I *should* go. I really should teach you a lesson and leave."

"Please, teach me," Mommy replied softly.

Grandmother Beverly looked at me and I looked down.

"Very well, I'll take one of those garden apartments where Mrs. Saks lives."

"Good choice," Mommy said and picked up her fork without skipping a beat.

"Taylor will be upset," Grandmother warned.

"Well, we'll tell him it's what you wanted, won't we?" Mommy asked her with a smile. "That way, we won't risk his being too upset, okay, Beverly? I know that's what you want too."

Grandmother Beverly pressed her lips together and nodded slowly.

"He married you against my wishes; he should suffer the consequences of his actions."

"We all do, Beverly," Mommy said. "We all suffer the consequences of our actions in the end."

I held my breath.

Grandmother Beverly rose, looked at us, and went to her room.

Two days later, she was moved out of the house, and a day after that, Daddy came home.

Despite all that had happened and all the commotion and tension, Mommy had remembered to sign and send in the letter of acceptance to Madame Senetsky. I was surprised when she told me.

I was worried, too, because Daddy had revealed the financial burden was his main concern. Madame Senetsky's school was twice as expensive as a private college and there would be other associated expenses as well.

One afternoon, almost a week after Daddy was home, I came home from school and saw he was sitting on a chaise longue out back, getting some sun. Mommy was still at the supermarket. I wandered out and sat across from him. He looked like he was sleeping, but he opened his eyes immediately.

"Hey," he said.

"Hey."

"How's it going? School's coming to an end."

"Uh-huh."

"Graduation is always an exciting time," he said. He stared ahead for a moment and then he looked at me. "I've got to tell you something, Cinnamon. When I was being taken into the operating room for the pacemaker, I had one great fear."

"What, Daddy?"

"That I would die without telling you something, something I had to tell and something I couldn't tell your mother. I was afraid of what it might do to her. I'm still afraid."

I held my breath.

"I did something wrong a while back and I had to work my way out of it. I'm ashamed of it, but I realize you're old enough to know that your father's not perfect. No one's perfect. When you're young, you can believe the people you love are perfect and that's fine. It makes the world seem safer, but you're about to go out into the real world, the competitive cold world and you'd better know it's not a walk in the sun."

"I know it isn't, Daddy."

"Yes, I think you're a much smarter, more mature young lady than most your age, and I've got to credit your mother for that. She's done a great job with you while I had my face buried in stocks and bonds."

He paused, looked away and then spoke softly.

"Some time ago, I used a client's investment money to speculate on a stock I was sure would have a very big return. It would have, if something hadn't come up that caused the Food and Drug Administration to call back the company's product. I lost most of the money and I had to confront the client and tell her."

"Her?"

"Yes. She's a wealthy woman, a widow. The reaction she had and what she wanted was quite unexpected. I was prepared to borrow on life insurance policies, the house, everything and anything, but she knew she had me in a box. What I did would cause me to lose my license and be thrown out on the street."

"What did she want, Daddy?"

"She wanted me to pretend . . . to pretend she was someone I admired . . . loved," he said. "She had a fantasy and I had to be part of it for a while. Finally, I was able to restore her funds and break loose of her hold on me." He shook his head. "Crazy thing is, she wasn't upset. She was satisfied and has gone on to another fantasy. She even still invests with my firm."

"Why did you tell me this, Daddy?"

"When I was faced with the possible end of my life, I felt I had to get it off my conscience. The other day when Grandmother Beverly visited me, she told me about an accusation you had made and that got me thinking. Why did you tell her that, Cinnamon?"

Now it was my turn to look away. He waited. Tears were building under my lids.

"One day I cut school . . ."

"Yes, I remember that."

"And Clarence Baron and I went to the city to spy on you. I thought you were trying to get another job or that you were in some financial trouble."

"I was."

194

"But that's not what I thought it was," I said. "I followed you to a coffee shop and saw you kiss a woman on the lips."

"Ah," he said. "You're not going to believe it, but I had the feeling I was being watched. Your mother's and your spirits," he muttered. "This house . . ." he said looking up. "So that was it."

"Yes, Daddy."

"Well, I'm glad we had this talk," he said. "I hate secrets between me and the people I love. I can only imagine how terrible you must have felt and how angry, but you couldn't have hated me more than I hated myself."

"I never hated you, Daddy," I said. "But I was angry."

"Sure. You should have been. I would have been, too. I say I hate secrets, but I don't see any good in telling your mother about this."

"That's up to you, Daddy, you and Mommy."

He nodded and smiled.

"You are very mature and very perceptive. I'm glad you're going to that school, Cinnamon."

"What about the cost?"

"Well," he said. "I had a good talk with your Grandmother Beverly and she agreed to free up your trust."

"She did?"

"Yes," he said laughing. "Your mother was right about her. She's happier living somewhere else, anywhere else but in this house," he said.

"Do you hate our house?"

"Hate it?" He thought a moment. "No. I used to be afraid of it, afraid those spirits of yours would get me. Maybe they did. I deserved it if they did. But, the place kind of grows on you," he said.

He rose.

"I'd better go in. Your mother will be home any moment and I want to help her."

"I'll be there, too."

"Naw, don't worry. We can handle it," he said. He stood there looking at me.

And I ran into his arms and we held each other for a long, precious moment.

"I love you, baby," he said. "And you make me proud, very, very proud."

He kissed my forehead and walked into the house.

I sucked in my breath and started for the hill. When I got there, I looked at the tombstones and then I rushed forward and pulled the stick out of the ground. I dug like a mad dog until I found my charm necklace, the one Daddy had given me. I brushed it off and put it back on quickly.

Then I looked at the stones once more, turned and walked back toward the house.

Toward the future.

Toward tomorrow when I would be on another stage in front of another audience.

Under the spotlight.

The employees of G.K. Hall hope you have enjoyed this Large Print book. All our Large Print titles are designed for easy reading, and all our books are made to last. Other G.K. Hall books are available at your library, through selected bookstores, or directly from us.

For information about titles, please call:

(800) 223-1244
(800) 223-6121

To share your comments, please write:

Publisher
G.K. Hall & Co.
295 Kennedy Memorial Drive
Waterville, ME 04901